In all directions

In all directions

16 Short Stories
from members of the
Canadian Authors Association
across the country

Edited and with an Introduction by
Bernice Lever
Foreword by Gillian M. Foss

Fitzhenry & Whiteside

Fitzhenry & Whiteside Limited
195 Allstate Parkway, Markham, Ontario L3R 4T8

In the United States (queries only):
121 Harvard Avenue, Suite 2, Allston, Massachusetts 02134

www.fitzhenry.ca
godwit@fitzhenry.ca

Fitzhenry & Whiteside acknowledges with thanks the support of the
Government of Canada through its Book Publishing Industry
Development Program.

The publisher gratefully acknowledges the support of The Canada
Council for the Arts for our publishing program.

Canadian Cataloguing in Publication Data

Main entry under title:
In all directions : 16 short stories from members of the Canadian
Authors Association across the country
ISBN 1-55041-608-1

1. Short Stories, Canadian (English).* 2. Canadian fiction (English) –
20th century.* I. Bernice Lever, 1936- . II. Canadian Authors Association.

PS8321.I63 2000   C813'.0108054   C00-930655-2
PR9197.32.I63 2000

Design by Karen Petherick/Intuitive Design Studio

Cover photograph: Digital Imagery® copyright 1999 PhotoDisc, Inc.

Printed and bound in Canada.

Contents

In All Directions is the latest anthology of work by members of the Canadian Authors Association and the project leading the organization into the new century.

This collection contains the winning entries from a country-wide contest, with one story chosen from each branch of the Association by an external judge. All members of the CAA, whether Voting or Associate, were eligible to enter. Stories from both groups appear in this book.

In 1921, the CAA was established to promote recognition of Canadian writers and their work; to protect authors' rights; to stimulate work of literary and artistic merit; and to improve the professionalism of Canadian writers. It continues to accomplish these goals by welcoming writers of all abilities and in all genres and encouraging members to develop their potential through networking at the local and national levels. Locally, beginners learn from the more experienced members at branch meetings, workshops and seminars. The national focus is an annual conference where participants attend seminars, discuss important issues, and mingle with top writers, editors, publishers and technical experts as well as fellow members.

In All Directions is a practical result of CAA's policies and speaks positively to the Association's motto of "Writers Helping Writers." For those members in the early stages of a writing career publication in this collection will bring greater recognition. For those already well established, it is one more attribute in a line of successes. In both these cases, *In All Directions* is proof that the Canadian Authors Association is still providing valuable service to the Canadian literary community.

Gillian M. Foss
National President

Canadian short story writers have been popular internationally for over a hundred years. Many foreign readers became interested in Canadian writers when Ernest Thompson Seton and Charles G.D. Roberts wrote stories of our animals and landscape spreading the natural appeals of our country at the beginning of the 20th century. Soon pirated copies of works by Canadian writers appeared in the USA and United Kingdom. To protect their copyrights, our Canadian writers banded together. Stephen Leacock, whose short humorous stories are still read worldwide, was one of the founding members of the Canadian Authors Association in 1921. Many famous Canadian writers began and/or continue with the CAA today, since splinter genre groups only started in the 1960s. Robert Munsch of Guelph, a fabulous writer of children's picture books, supports the CAA as does Cora Taylor of Edmonton, a past National CAA President who has written prize-winning stories for young adults. Today, past CAA fiction winners Alice Munro, W.P. Kinsella, W.D. Valgardson, and many others are now winning international prizes for their short stories in several genres.

Now for the next century, these sixteen CAA members from coast to coast present their winning stories. Each local branch held a short story contest to select the best story that told one part of Canada's current concerns and hopes. Also represented are "members-at-large" who do not have a local branch affiliation.

These stories are about what matters in people's lives: births, deaths, earthquakes, self-worth, secrets and laughs, love lost and love found. These writers bring the major emotions, values and human ties to vibrant reality. Given the diversity of our nation and its writers, all readers will find one voice or more in this collection that speaks to them. Multicultural Canada is very much evident in these stories set in Italy, Wales, India and other countries, or in one of the many cultures that feed the richness of our literature.

This anthology has stories one can share with teen readers. They will laugh with the antics of boys trying secretly to smoke or at the descriptions of unusual funeral homes and hearses. They may even shed a tear with characters struggling through family divorces and their attendant feelings of confusion and alienation.

Several stories mark the miracle passages of life from birth to death. Mothers-to-be support each other with the help of an "angel," a popular figure in today's books and TV programs. Other stories explore the loss of family members — even partners — with all that pain, denial and other roller-coaster reactions.

Some stories depict a nostalgia for a "love lost," or emphasize the power of "first lovers." Many of these tales focus on discovering one's self-worth and identity in life's struggles and relationships. A science fiction "what-if" plot defines our humanity as life continues into the millennium, while life today is made special as lively fantasy replaces dull, lonely routines.

How Canadian to find hope and goodness in so many varied voices! These sixteen CAA writers deserve our close reading attention to their well-expressed words. As the editor privileged to birth this anthology, I can announce, "The Canadian short story is alive and well!"

Bernice Lever

REINVENTING ALICE MUNRO

Mrs. Moodie studied her makeshift easel, applied a final swirl of viridian green and stood back. Not much like Emily Carr's but it would do. The totem pole was a bit askew, its rendering more like a happy-face than the fierce icons that her predecessor painted. The trees, on close scrutiny, resembled tipsy sun umbrellas. No matter. Being Emily Carr for a month had been fun but today was April 30th, the finale for long skirts, headbands and her Reeves jumbo set of beginner's oils. Tomorrow Mrs. Moodie would be someone else.

Alice Munro.

A year ago, at eighty, Mrs. Moodie had faced the fact that she was never going to be famous in her own right. Years of office cleaning and penny-scrounging widowhood haunted her. It was time to live a little, before it was too late. Why not borrow fame? Get inside a different celebrity's skin each month, live as she did. Do a little re-inventing, if necessary. She'd always wanted to dabble in arty things — to inhale the success that famous writers, artists and entertainers enjoyed.

She set few guidelines for choosing an idol to model herself on. Female, living or dead. A household name. A stickler for Canadian content, she rejected, regretfully, Maria Callas and Elizabeth Taylor.

1

By moving to a bachelor walk-up, she saved enough money to buy the trappings to indulge her fantasies: paint tubes, typewriter ribbons, second-hand books, an occasional ticket, seniors' rate, to a relevant lecture or film.

May was going to be the high point of all her transformations. On the 31st, Alice Munro would give a public reading at the National Library. Mrs. Moodie had managed to get on the invitation list. Never before had she had the chance to see and hear, first hand, the very personality she had adopted.

Lifting the canvas off its easel, she recalled her more memorable adventures. She'd broken her ankle being Barbara Ann Scott, not having skated for years. She'd been laid up over Christmas and forced to cancel January. Celine Dion was beyond her, her French wasn't good enough, but her Anne Murray stint had been loads of fun. She had sashayed around her apartment, holding an unplugged extension cord to her lips, belting out "Snowbird" every morning before breakfast until she was sure she had it right. The neighbours upstairs had complained. Fortunately for them it was February, the shortest month.

"Tomorrow I'm Alice Munro," she sang to herself as she cleaned her brushes. Already she saw herself as petite and slender, with a hint of humour in her steady gaze. She had heard that celebrities spoke with authority and biting wit, so she had begun to walk taller, to stride forth on outings using her cane more as jaunty accessory than support. She demanded leaner cuts at the butcher's, refusing to pay for even a morsel of fat. She snapped at her hairdresser, quite alarming poor Mildred, who had steadfastly indulged her styling whims without comment.

Tomorrow, May 1st, she would go to Mildred and demand a perm like Alice Munro's, short and curly. With a dark rinse, of course, although the cover photo on *Selected Stories* showed a woman with hair as white as her own. She had already bought dangly earrings — paid a hefty price, in fact, to get a pair just like the ones in Alice's ears. The pearl teardrops flattered the face regarding her from the glossy book jacket. Mrs. Moodie hoped the imitations wouldn't give the impression of making her own jawline sag. The earrings reminded Mrs.

Moodie of her long-lost Jacqui, although they were much classier than the dimestore jewellery Jacqui treasured. Mrs. Moodie had a mental picture of Jacqui, age nineteen, getting up in the morning, tiny silvery stars tinkling against her neck. The girl never took them off, nor did she remove her makeup at night. Mornings she looked as if she had two black eyes. Mrs. Moodie wiped her easel and took up the plastic sheet that protected the floor. Then she folded the easel, hoping to fold away her memories of Jacqui with it.

Fearing that others would think she was in her dotage, she kept her little game a secret. She had no trouble distinguishing reality from fantasy, thank goodness! She shivered inside the paint-daubed smock she'd fashioned out of Mr. Moodie's wedding shirt. It was hard sometimes to fool herself, peering into the mirror at white hair and wrinkles, anchoring her reading glasses while struggling to apply lipstick.

Jacqui, her only child, had been born when she was a teenager, long before she had married Mr. Moodie. The product of a liaison she blushed to remember, the neighbourhood boy who'd taken her to the grad dance. They'd hardly known each other, really, but someone had spiked their Cokes, and then, because it was such a hot night, they'd each had a second, also spiked, and since he'd borrowed his father's car, they'd gone for a drive to cool off. One thing had led to another. Looking back, she realized she'd been lucky that the two sets of formidable parents, each pointing fingers of blame at their offspring's unfortunate choice of partner, hadn't forced them to marry. The boy had gone off to college and graduated in some program she'd never heard of, and the last word she'd had, decades ago, he'd settled in some foreign country that had changed its name.

The child, whom she named Marigold, had been adopted by a local family and renamed Jacqui. Shortly afterwards, they'd moved to Kapuskasing, and she'd lost touch with them. Then, not long after she had married Mr. Moodie, Jacqui, now a teenager, had come looking for her. Before she knew it, the girl had moved into the spare bedroom, almost destroying the Moodies' fledgling marriage. Fortunately, Mr. Moodie was broad-minded and took the news of the girl's parentage in his stride. Nevertheless, Jacqui caused endless problems, smuggling her boyfriend in nightly and drinking all the liquor in Mr. Moodie's cabinet. An elfish girl with a curiously perverse charm, she constantly quarreled with her mother, borrowed her clothes without asking and sometimes helped herself to the bills in Mrs. Moodie's purse. When she began flirting with her new step-father, Mrs. Moodie realized she had to assert herself. She reminded herself that she had made her choices about the girl long ago. With tears in her eyes, she helped Jacqui pack and walked her to the bus station. "Go home," she said, aware that "home" was beyond her imagination. She pressed her rent money into Jacqui's hand, hugged her and walked away. After a week of halcyon relief, Mrs. Moodie realized she had set herself up for a lifetime of self-recrimination.

Once she thought she saw the girl on the street, heavily made up, in a leather skirt about the size of a postage stamp and a skintight top with a scandalous neckline. She was dragging on a cigarette and chatting up a couple of young men with greasy hair and bad teeth. Was it Jacqui? The thought robbed her of countless nights of sleep.

In bed on the eve of her Alice Munro gig — that was how she thought of it — Mrs. Moodie tossed and turned. Despite years of agonizing guilt, she had never once tried to locate Jacqui. She couldn't bring herself to. But dreams, waking and sleeping, and uncertain sightings, although less frequent, persisted. Less believable, they became somehow more magical and easier to bear.

She closed her eyes and tried to woo sleep with flowers, whole gardens of them. But it was geraniums that appeared tonight, reminding her of her long-ago attempts to brighten up the first Moodie home. And suddenly a flower pot came hurling at her, she saw it clearly in the darkness, shattering and leaving its petals like drops of blood all over her kitchen floor. Jacqui again, another bad memory. She got up, pattered to her kitchenette and made camomile tea. She sat in her armchair, sipping.

Mr. Moodie had died three years after their marriage, leaving her penniless. She went back to cleaning offices, working long past retirement age. Evenings, she read classics. "Keep my brain from turning to oatmeal," she told herself. Now, her eyes beginning to droop at last, she tottered to bed and began to snore her way gently into a dreamless sleep.

The 1st of May arrived with the unexpected threat of a heat wave. It was her habit to lie in bed for a while when she awakened at daybreak, planning her day. Alice Munro, she decided, would write for an hour or two on rising, so anxious would she be to fashion her wonderful stories. Breakfast would be modest, toast and coffee. Alice Munro would shower and dress, fluffing up her damp, cooperative hair. Then she would make a pie.

The rest of Alice's day was probably spent on the phone, accepting speaking engagements and dining invitations. Since Mrs. Moodie's phone seldom rang, she decided to use the time rereading Alice's books and writing pretend letters: Dear —. Thank you for my most recent award. I am running out of space in my trophy room....

The sunlight streaming across her pillow, Mrs. Moodie rose, went to her desk, and sat down at her typewriter. It was going to be a hectic month. She planned to write four short stories, one a week, using her Alice Munro books for guidance.

Several months ago she had listened to a radio program — more like a love-in, actually — where a fellow had been interviewing Alice but did most of the talking himself. He had gone on and on about lemon meringue pie. Mrs. Moodie couldn't remember his exact words, but it seemed that Alice Munro had made a lemon meringue pie that was the pinnacle of culinary success, just as her books were literary sensations. Now she'd do the same: learn to make the best lemon meringue pie in the world.

In the ensuing days, Mrs. Moodie had more success with the pie than the stories. By the third week, after a generous wedge with her tea each noon, her enthusiasm for lemon meringue palled. More upsetting, though, her writing wasn't going well at all. She felt like Camus's character in *The Plague*, the one who kept rewriting the same opening sentence to his novel.

Write what you know! She'd heard that somewhere. Well, what did she know? How to clean people's toilets, vacuum hairs from carpets, make leftovers stretch.

Boring! Could she make a story about the time she cleaned nail polish off her boss's oak desk — what was it doing there, anyway? — or the time she found a bracelet in her popcorn container at the theatre? Or her bus trip to Peterborough when that nice young honeymoon couple had asked her to settle an argument? She shuddered. This was her life.

What about Mr. Moodie? She could barely remember him, let alone write about him. A taciturn man, he had smoked his pipe and read his newspaper, following baseball and the stock markets with equal fervour but never betting on either.

So much for Mr. Moodie. There had been no one after him. Neighbours, seeing her hurrying off to the library each evening, would hint at a clandestine affair. "There's not exactly a line-up at my door," she would say with a little laugh. The neighbour women, pausing with hedge clippers or shopping bags, would smile knowingly.

But it was true; there was no one. She'd never been pretty, never good at small talk. How young women these days chatted up their fellows she could never fathom. But there they were, all around her, these young Jacquis, on the streets, hanging onto a youth's arm, or in theatres, openly kissing and running their hands, well, all over. Looking smug and proprietary, the way only men used to. She couldn't write about those things; they weren't her life.

It had been different with Mr. Moodie, though hardly exciting. He was widowed, and several years older. He'd come around trying to sell her a vacuum cleaner and she'd turned a lot of business his way, since she cleaned so many offices. "Your old vacuum's not picking up the lint so well," she'd tell her employers. "There's this nice salesman..." After he'd sold five machines on her recommendations, he'd dropped in one morning without his demonstrator model and suggested lunch. Twelve Tuesday lunches later, he'd proposed.

She sighed. Getting married had meant moving into his seedy rental, where no amount of vacuuming and polishing could make the place cheerful. She'd hung geranium baskets in every window and put all her precious knickknacks on the mantle above the boarded-up fireplace. When she thought of Mr. Moodie, she remembered rustling newspaper, a dry cough, and clothes permeated with tobacco smoke.

Not the stuff of Alice Munro. She turned to Jacqui: could she write about her? The one wild card in her life. The only thing that had happened to her, and it had been a mistake, a disaster. She thought of the day her baby was born, the pink cheeks so delicate they were almost transparent, the tiny hand curling around her finger. She'd never got to keep a scrapbook of first steps and cute sayings. No smocking little dresses or choosing pink satin hair ribbons. No bronzed baby shoes to hang on the wall.

Should she put an ad in the paper? "Jacqui, born Marigold Jones, please contact your mother at —" But Jacqui would be sixty-two. Mrs. Moodie didn't know her last name, didn't know if she ever knew she'd been Marigold.

Mrs. Moodie kept visualizing a young woman with short brown hair, ever-so-slightly bent, not curled, on the ends, and always with those dangly earrings. What would she look like now? What if Mrs. Moodie's thoughts recoiled. She didn't even know if Jacqui were alive.

May sped by. The pie became a *cause célèbre* when she invited a local reading group to meet at her place. She spent hours each day walking, sitting on park benches reading *Lives of Girls and Women*. Her own stories, however, refused to take shape on the page. Well, I don't have to write quite like Alice, Mrs. Moodie thought. Perhaps I should write about what I don't know, or write a story in the form of a letter, or start with a list. She tried these ploys, to no avail. Everything she wrote sounded awkward, amateurish. And by page three her idea, whatever it was, dried up.

On the last day of May, without a single story finished, she took a bus downtown to the Delta Inn near the National Library. She would treat herself to supper in the restaurant before Alice's reading. She felt good about herself, her hair permed and darkly tinted. She went for the understated look, sure that Alice Munro would approve. Plain black dress, a single strand of imitation pearls that could possibly be real, if one didn't look closely.

The waiter's mask of politeness hardly slipped at all as Mrs. Moodie twirled her cane, just once, in the doorway. He motioned her to a seat behind a wall that had a space the shape of a keyhole cut in it. Her earrings trembled excitedly. You belong, they told her. You're a celebrity.

She ordered the cream soup, which arrived scalding hot, saltier than her doctor would have approved but just the way she liked it. The accompanying tuna sandwich bulged until its filling oozed onto her plate. She began blotting up bits with her index finger.

Wouldn't it be wonderful if Alice Munro were dining here, she thought. All by herself. Wouldn't it be the thrill of a lifetime if I got to speak to her? But no, Alice Munro, the famous author, would be feted by admirers, probably at a banquet put on by those patrons of the arts who arrange such things. She would be dining on fillet mignon at the head of a long table while worshipping eyes watched as each forkful was raised to her lips. Mrs. Moodie stopped blotting up tuna crumbs, picked up her knife and fork and began cutting tiny cubes from her sandwich, putting her fork to her mouth with finesse and chewing delicately. Just as if a whole restaurant-full of people was watching.

She was mulling over the idea of ordering the cheesecake when she happened to glance through the keyhole into the adjacent dining room. She couldn't believe it!

There sat Alice Munro, at a table. Alone. In fact, she was the only person in that entire dining room. Mrs. Moodie pushed her glasses up on her nose. Yes, it was Alice, no mistake about it. A calm, ordinary woman, looking perhaps as Mrs. Moodie herself had looked a couple of decades earlier. Unassuming. That was the word. Alice Munro was unassuming. Approachable, even. Mrs. Moodie took a deep breath. She left enough money on her table to pay her bill, and a modest tip for the waiter, picked up her purse and cane and headed for the door leading into Alice Munro's dining room.

The object of her adulation was leafing through papers while a half-eaten dinner congealed on her plate.

"Excuse me," Mrs. Moodie said. "You're Alice Munro, aren't you?" The woman nodded.

"I hope you don't mind. You see, I'm a fan — perhaps your greatest fan, ever. I just had to come up and — and — ."

Alice Munro didn't look annoyed. She didn't look acerbic or impatient. She certainly didn't look as if she would tell her butcher off or make impossible demands on her hairdresser.

"I didn't expect to find you alone," Mrs. Moodie blurted. She held out her hand and introduced herself. She hesitated, cleared her throat and added, "I'm a writer. Yes. I'm a writer, too."

Alice Munro put down a sheaf of papers and held out her hand to Mrs. Moodie's. Her voice was soft. "I've been sitting here trying to decide which story to read. I've narrowed it down to two," she said. "I can't decide whether to read my earlier one," she gestured with the papers in her left hand, "or this one that I just finished." She nodded toward the pile deposited dangerously close to her coleslaw.

Mrs. Moodie was dumb-founded. Was Alice Munro asking for advice? "I'm sure either one will be great," Mrs. Moodie said. "Perhaps you won't know until you see the audience. You know, get a feel for their mood." She wasn't sure such a thing was possible, but she had to say something. Something that sounded as if she knew from experience. "I'll be there." She blushed at the reassuring note in her voice. What difference would it make to Alice Munro, who wouldn't remember her five minutes from now?

Alice consulted her watch and shoved her papers into her briefcase. "I have to go," she said. "I have to slip into the National Library before they open the doors to the public." She smiled apologetically. "I hope you enjoy the reading."

Tucking her cane under her arm, Mrs. Moodie fumbled in her purse for pen and paper. She scribbled her name and address on the back of an old envelope and handed it over. "Just in case you'd ever like to chat. In case," she steadied herself with her cane, "you, uh, might see my name somewhere, some day."

Her legs were wobbling like jelly as she crossed to the Library. A lineup had formed already; by the time she got into the auditorium, she had to sit near the back.

The woman sitting beside her was about sixty. She had short grey hair, bent just a little on the ends, and silvery earrings that dangled almost to her shoulders. She had a kind, open face and a breezy way of laughing.

"You like Alice Munro?" Mrs. Moodie asked her. She needed to engage the woman in conversation, to see if it was possible even to imagine that she might be Jacqui.

"Never heard of her before tonight," the woman said. "But my friend here, he's a CanLit buff." She poked a mustachioed gentleman on her left. "You're a real fan, aren't you, Herb." The man, his nose in a copy of *The Moons of Jupiter*, glanced up briefly and nodded. She turned back to Mrs. Moodie. "Educating me, he is," she said. Mrs. Moodie tried without success to edit out the woman's English accent. Pity. She looked so much as Mrs. Moodie imagined Jacqui would, though a bit on the heavy side. Perhaps Jacqui'd spent the last few decades in England. How long did it take to acquire an accent?

The lights dimmed and Alice Munro, looking unassuming, vulnerable even, walked onto the stage. Mrs. Moodie wanted to hug her, give her a few words of assurance. "Take heart, dear," she'd say. Then Alice started to read in a calm, clear voice. Mental telepathy, Mrs. Moodie thought, she got my message.

The story was a wonderful one about parents' stormy relationships with teenagers and how people thought one thing and said another, then regretted not saying what they thought. Mrs. Moodie couldn't follow it very well because she was aware of the woman beside her, the possible Jacqui. The woman's earrings tinkled distractingly and she laughed in inappropriate places. Her escort sat glumly, staring hard at Alice as if scrutinizing her more closely would help him to hear better. Mrs. Moodie was disappointed that her spiritual union with Alice, so real, so gratifying, had been disturbed, but surely her daughter, her own long-lost child, was more important. She had to know — didn't she?

Afterward, even before the applause died down, the couple beside her pushed their way outside. Mrs. Moodie couldn't keep up with them. The man, Herb, was explaining something to his companion, a line from *Lives of Girls and Women* where the main character says that a writer's only duty is to produce a masterpiece and how, when she got older, Alice Munro herself didn't accept that view any more. The woman forged on ahead, plainly not listening. "Wait up, Jan," Herb called. "Let's go for a beer."

Jan. Perhaps Jacqui had changed her name, kept just the initial. Mrs. Moodie clutched her purse as the crowd pressed around her. She was mother to all these possible Jacquis — legions of them! They kept her imagination — or was it her quest for identity? — alive. Dear Jacqui. Wherever she was, she would have made it on her own, and, with a little luck, had some good times, too. Perhaps when Jacqui was eighty-one she wouldn't have to become someone else to find a reason for going on.

Mrs. Moodie jabbed her cane at an abandoned gum wrapper. Perhaps she didn't, either. But being someone else had become part of being herself! "Life's what you make it," she murmured, aware of a resolute banality that reminded her she wasn't a writer, not a great one, anyway. No new stories, she thought, just what you make of the old ones. In making something of them, you become your own story.

Of course, that's it!

In bed that night, Mrs. Moodie took stock of May. Being Alice Munro had been exhausting! She closed her eyes and let flowers spring up in her mind. This time they were restful little sprigs, forget-me-nots, lilies-of-the-valley, dotting a sweeping green meadow. Sleep wouldn't elude her tonight.

Next month, if her joints didn't protest too much, she'd try something really daring: Karen Kain. Already she was mentally haunting the shops, looking for tulle and tights, a *Swan Lake* tape. And those dear little pointy-toed slippers that ballerinas wore: could she make a pair? And afterward, have them bronzed and hang them in her kitchenette window, dangling from pink satin ribbon?

PLUTONIC ROCK

Just simply alive,

Both of us, I

and the poppy.

Issa

Mona trailed a hand through the poppy bed. Only one huge branch had dropped off an oak tree she noticed; otherwise, this section of their condominium's oak meadow backyard, which she maintained, looked undamaged. She moved past a clump of raspberries, eating a few. Birds chirped, and a swallowtail butterfly flitted. She saw a new little blackberry seedling and pulled it. "In two years, this garden will be overgrown with broom and brambles again." She spoke aloud.

"For six years, I've told them that this garden, developed, will be a haven of food and repose if disaster strikes." She looked around. "I'm a senior; I get free ferry trips to and from Vancouver Mondays to Thursdays. I can camp here overnight; like the Soviets do at their dachas."

She looked up at the condominium building on the hill above.

It appeared as solid as before, but there was a crack in the living room wall and the sign on the door warned of structural damage. She broke off a pink somniferum poppy blossom, admired it, then turned towards the rock outcropping in the far back corner of her clearing. She felt calmer, and revived a little, just being down here.

She walked up onto the rock, retrieved a little board from the crevice it had slid into, positioned it in her favourite spot and sat on it. This was plutonic rock she reminded herself. It formed when the earth's crust formed. It's old; it bears glacier scars. It had been a special find when she cleared blackberry bushes. She laid a hand on the rock, felt its warmth, and the slight roughness. "Somewhere nearby there will be a rift in the rock on Vancouver Island from this earthquake. But not here." She caressed it. "We have survived a lot. You and I and the poppies."

Mona's eyes focused on a distant, more common, field poppy. She remembered her and Chris parking the car under the library, and heading across the street to the Brighton Centre. As they approached the old building, the sidewalk heaved. She staggered out across the sidewalk, and doubled over the engine of a car parked at the curb.

"Whoa!" Chris yelled, staggering off in the opposite direction. She saw him grab for the corner of the building, but it dumped him reeling backwards around the corner. The ground kept heaving and bucking. She saw the brick wall of the building coming down on Chris.

The heaving ground pounded a yell out of her. It just kept heaving in big waves. Her feet, working with the waves, moved her around to the far side of the car, and staggering out into the street. The wall kept falling down. Bricks bounced off cars with a great banging. Then the front corner of the building crashed outwards. The windows broke. Dust and noise filled the air, and over and above and beyond the immediate noise was a loud roar, the likes of which she had never heard before.

A moving car nudged her, backing her up a few steps before it stopped. She spread her hands on the engine, and looked over to where Chris had been. The ground suddenly stopped heaving. "Chris?" she called.

People came out of the building, stepping over rubble, crying, whimpering, yelling and helping each other. Cars kept rolling in and stopping. More people emerged and filled the street. They were subdued at first. They moved slowly about, asking each other if they were all right.

"My husband!"

Mona grabbed at a man, and pushed and pulled him towards where Chris had been. She pulled him a few steps, then the man stopped them. They stared at the ugly gaping inner corner of the building. The innards of the copy and printing shop showed. On the sidewalk was a huge pile of debris. "My husband!" Mona whimpered in near hysterics.

A siren, unlike any siren Mona had heard before, was sounding from somewhere near them. It was so loud it vibrated her voice when she yelled. Another clatter sounded. They grabbed each other, and stared beyond the building to the dropping brick wall of a building at the back of the parking lot. Someone on the west side shouted "Get out of here!" Mona saw people being pushed and moving out of the walkway beside that building. More bricks, one at a time, and from up at the top of the building beside them, came dropping down.

People were then galvanized into talk and action. Mona moved between two cars over closer to where Chris should have been. Bricks from the wall were piled the height of the hood of the car. A police siren blared. Mona hurried forward, picked a brick off Chris, and dropped it onto the pile on the sidewalk.

"Watch out!" a man yelled.

"My husband!" she yelled with the vibrating tremor in her voice. She was pulled back. Men crowded in and heaved bricks.

"Who else?" A man was holding her, shaking her gently, and yelling in her ear.

"I don't know." she replied.

Whomp! A great resounding boom sounded in the west. People

jumped, screamed and stared westward. The large church across the corner where the street curved off at an angle was still standing, but a great horde of people were running across the intersection toward them. The men heaving the bricks off the pile on Chris jumped and staggered back over the debris away from the building. Mona heard a ripping, squeaking sound.

A policeman arrived. A man grabbed his sleeve, pulled him west, babbling to him. A big dark cloud was mushrooming up beyond the church. The ground heaved again. People cried out, walloped around, leaned on cars and staggered. A cracking and clapping sounded to the west. Mona watched a portion of the old brick wall on the west side of the parking lot collapse.

"Turn gas off!...electricity and water...Don't go in there!" Voices shouted around her.

"The earthquake must have been right under us." a woman said to Mona. "I lived through this in San Francisco." Another siren sounded close at hand. A car horn blared behind Mona. The driver in a car facing west, stood up beside his car and yelled and motioned for people behind him to back their cars eastward. "They have to get emergency vehicles through this street!" He yelled at them.

The cars on the far side of the street, and facing east, edged slowly along. Another Whomp! echoed in the west. Another huge dark cloud of smoke billowed up.

Chris's foot was uncovered. A man felt for a pulse and reflexes around his ankle. A larger pile of debris had to be removed from the rest of his body. Mona moved in closer. "Get back!" one of the men yelled at her. He swung his arm backwards, hitting her across the chest. "You gotta stay back!"

"My husband!" Mona yelled shakily.

Sirens were blaring constantly now, and black smoke was wafting toward them.

The men cleared the rest of Chris's body. He lay on his back, contorted, mangled, bleeding, and dirty. His face was such a bloody mess that Mona couldn't see the features on it. The man tried to find a pulse. Mona tried to stifle her crying and screaming while a couple of people cradled her in their arms and tried to turn her away from the gruesome sight of Chris.

"Does he have a wallet?" the man asked. "They'll need identification."

Another man removed Chris's wallet from his pocket and held it out to Mona. There was wet blood on it. Mona stared at it in revulsion. Two of the men searched through his wallet and removed a driver's license. One man wiped the wallet with a tissue and tried handing it to Mona again. "You've got to take it." he said, opening her purse, putting it inside, then closing her purse again.

"No!" Mona heard herself say.

"Do you have a car handy?" the man asked her.

"Un-der the li-brar-y."

"The sprinklers are on." another said. "They have to block that. Cars have been coming out wet. People are still going in. God knows how bad the damage is."

Mona stood beside Chris's body. At times, she reeled in a near collapse. Other times, she just cried, and tried to answer people who asked questions and offered comfort. When stretcher bearers lifted his body she asked where they were taking him. She couldn't understand what they said. She followed them to the ambulance, and asked again. They shut the rear door, hurried to the cab, and told her to check it out tomorrow. The siren on the ambulance whooped and wailed. People parted and it moved off.

Mona stood there crying. Others ignored her now. She looked across at the library parking lot and saw two cars blocking the entrance and the exit lanes. A barricade and yellow tape blocked the sidewalk leading down into it. Foul smelling smoke was now in the air. People and cars were packed on the street. Mona struggled through the crowd, turned the corner and walked north: the direction of home.

A man was offering paper cups of water from a cooler. He put one in Mona's hand. "What's wrong with you?' he spoke with an accent. Mona drank the water. She forced herself to tell him that her husband had been killed.

The man put a hand on her arm. "A lot of people are probably dead. This is surely a nine on the scale."

A waitress came out of the door beside him carrying a tray loaded with sandwiches and muffins. They put a muffin in Mona's hand. "Where is your home?" the man asked.

"Up beyond McKenzie and Shelbourne."

"Here in Victoria?"

"Y-es."

"How did you get downtown?"

"Our car is under the library. They've blocked it."

"Walk home! You can't stay downtown tonight. Get out of here! I've lived through a war, with everything burning and crashing around me. I know! Tomorrow you do what you have to do! Tonight you go home and sleep in a lawn chair, or on the front lawn if you must lay down. Be glad you've got a home to go to. None of the hotels will be open. Downtown will be full of tourists with no beds to sleep in tonight!"

An old man took her elbow and moved her along. "Walk north to Johnson. Your bus to McKenzie and Shelbourne goes east on Johnson, then north on Shelbourne. Just follow that route. If the bus comes along, take it. If you have to walk, then rest in bus stops."

There were no traffic lights operating. Mona walked over and around debris on the sidewalks. She stared at the wrecked buildings as she passed them. Others walked out in the street, so she finally moved out into the street, too. At times, she found herself sandwiched between cars moving in different directions. She came to Johnson Street, turned east and wove her way through the traffic. She walked on noticing that her feet hurt; she wasn't wearing good walking shoes. No buses came along. She tried not to draw attention to her crying.

The setting sun behind her made the immediate surroundings look beautiful at one point. It seemed incongruous. She sat at a bus stop, removed her shoes and rubbed her feet. The brick wall collapsing down, and Chris's glasses pushed into the bloodied mess of his face filled her mind. She remembered the mural that had been on the wall. She remembered men clearing bricks and debris off Chris. She remembered the ambulance taking him away. Over and over and over, she remembered it.

People moved both ways on the sidewalk and streets, or just stood staring around. Mona walked on. She passed one bus stop, then had to sit at the next one to ease her hurting feet. It got dark but no street lights came on. Some people held lanterns and flashlights. Oncoming car lights hurt her eyes, and after their passing the darkness seemed darker and the debris on the sidewalk harder to see. The tears flooding her eyes added to the problem.

The curve north on the route was completely blocked with downed trees and hydro poles. A tape was strung across the street and both sidewalks. Mona back-tracked and turned down a narrower side street. She felt fear prickle at this change of route through a completely strange neighbourhood, and wondered if her purse would be stolen or if she would get lost. She felt relief when she got on to Shelbourne Street again. Her feet hurt with every step now, and she stopped at every bus stop to relieve them.

She walked up their panhandle driveway, a long, steep, tree-lined one, noticing that no one was about, and that the driveway lights weren't on. She thought about what she must tell the kids. A sheet of paper was stuck to the outside door. Her key worked in the lock, and the door opened as usual. She entered the dark foyer, crossed it and faced the inner hallway. Greater darkness and a musty warmth struck additional fear in her. One feeble emergency light shone in the opposite direction she had to go. The emergency lights were only supposed to last two hours she remembered. She stopped and became acutely aware of the blood pounding in her ears, and of her heavy breathing. She feared the building might collapse or burn.

She leaned against the inner hall wall feeling totally exhausted. Her feet pained beyond the point of walking any further. She cried aloud as she took her shoes off. She thought of her armchair just a little further down the hall, and of her bed, and of a drink of water. She forced herself to move. She put a hand on the wall in the greater darkness of the hallway here, felt the stucco wall, the fire hose compartment, more stucco, then her door. In the blackness, she felt several keys before finding the right one, then fumbled at the lock until it was inserted. She hobbled through, closed and locked the door and whimpered out loud again. She felt on the wall for the light switch. No light responded.

She saw the faint light from the spare bedroom window which lay ahead but just off to one side of the hallway. She passed the bathroom door, then the storage closet, then she saw the stronger light of the night sky coming through their bedroom window off left.

Chris kept a flashlight on the floor on his side of the bed she remembered. She forgot to feel with her feet, stepped on a book and slid. Fear shot through her. She stumbled forward over tissue boxes and books until her hands and legs hit the softness of the bed. She crawled up the length of it to sit with the pillows at her back. She breathed raggedly and trembled. She groped her way under the quilt and sheet. She remembered the flashlight, crawled over in the bed, reached down and felt around for it.

Everything loose in the room was on the floor. The books in the bookcase on her side of the bed were on the floor. The clock radio was on the floor, and no red light blinked the seconds. She shone the flashlight out through the bedroom door and saw that their high Queen Anne curio cabinet had tipped forward to lean against the opposite wall of the hall.

She remembered her watch. It was 1:35 AM. The flashlight was dim; she turned it off and sat in the darkness thinking frantically of all that had happened and of what she must now do. She turned the flashlight on again and walked over and around clutter to the bathroom. She remembered not to flush. She turned the cold water tap on and managed to get a glass of water to drink.

Mona woke to daylight and silence. She turned in the bed, closed her eyes again, and the happenings of the day before filled her mind. She went to the bathroom and saw yesterday's mascara was a mess around her eyes.

Mona glanced into the computer room; everything that could possibly fall was on the floor. In the hallway, she crouched under the curio cabinet and pushed it back upright, leaving the mess of ornaments laying as they were in it. In the living room and dining room, cabinet doors were open and the contents from everything were strewn on the floor. The cabinets themselves were bolted to the walls, but they hadn't put earthquake safety latches on the doors. She walked to the kitchen in the darkened end of the condo. Everything from the counters and cupboards seemed to be on the floor. She nudged broken dishes aside with a foot, put the toaster and teakettle back up on one counter, and the big microwave convection oven back up on another. She pushed the fridge back into position, then opened it and peered into the darkened interior. She found the jug of filtered water, and her vitamin pills. She found the half loaf of bread on the floor, then searched the fridge for cheese, lettuce and margarine.

In the living room, she saw a long ragged crack in one wall and another in the ceiling. She heard a car door shut and looked out. She didn't recognize the couple walking up to the front door. She stayed well back out of sight; she knew she shouldn't be in here, but she was here, she reasoned, and wanted to stay here for a while. The people left, and Mona thought she should knock on neighbours' doors. She used precious stored water to wash. She put on fresh make-up and fresh clothes.

She got no response when she knocked on the doors along the dark hallway. The glass in the windows on both sides of the front door were cracked, but they hadn't fallen out. The note said that there was structural damage, and that it was forbidden to enter the building. It encouraged people to leave notes. No one had.

She walked back through the dark hallway to her condo, sat in an armchair and stared out of the patio doors. They were broken though still partially intact. The earthquake and Chris's death were all that filled her mind. She felt alone and confused.

She found the metal box containing their important papers, found the bankbook, a list of addresses and a stack of business cards in the oak roll-top desk and put them into the metal box. She found herself shaking violently and crying jerkily. Chris was gone!

In the late evening, she listlessly and weakly stacked books, and put broken dishes and ornaments into an empty clothes hamper. Her broken treasures elicited little grief she noticed. At other times, she would have been angry and upset. "They'll demolish this," she said aloud.

No lights came on. She lit candles, made herself a tuna sandwich and a salad, and finished off her supper with a banana. Her nose stung, and her eyes felt inflamed and gritty from crying. She packed clothes for herself in two suitcases. She tried heating water over the fondue candle to make tea, but gave up waiting for it to boil so steeped the tea in warm water. It was weak but tolerably good. She wondered why they had never bothered to buy a small propane burner. That thought-lessness angered her now.

She tried to plan the next day. She realized she should have gone out today to notify the kids, to find people to talk to and to start processing their affairs as one has to do when a spouse dies. The day had just passed by on her. She didn't know where to go first. Some places she would have to go were spread out about the city, and she didn't have the car. If she walked, she had no guarantee the places she needed to go to would be open for business. She felt torn between the desire to be with people she knew, and a strong desire to stay here at home for as long as she could. The thought of leaving the condo filled her with the anxiety of not being sure she would be allowed back in once she left.

Late in the night, she brought the quilt out to the living room and sat in her armchair with the flashlight on her lap. She dozed, then woke with a jerk when her head dropped. She stared out into the starlit night. Again, the beauty seemed incongruous after the devastation. She dozed, then jerked awake again. She wept quietly, dozed, jerked awake, shifted in the chair and dozed. She listened always for creaking sounds and strained to smell smoke.

Then it was daylight. "I have to make a start today," she said out loud as she moved out of her armchair. Talking aloud to herself startled her, but it felt good, too. "I can't take my suitcases with me. I'll have to take a couple of bags. And wear my exercise shoes," she mumbled while she prepared breakfast. "They have to allow people in to gather up their stuff. They probably will today." She kept listening and watching for someone to come, but no one came. She decided to go to her garden, for what might be the last time for quite some time. She would have to go over to Vancouver to stay with Trevor and Janice. She wrote a note and stuck it on the paper on the front door saying she was down in her clearing in the backyard.

Movement caught her eye. Mona blinked, then called. "Trevor!"

"Mom!"

They clung to each other. "I saw Dad," Trevor said, his voice breaking.

"Yeah." Mona replied and cried. "It was so gawd-awful."

"We felt the earthquake in Vancouver. It was so strong I thought the main earthquake was under us. It's an unbelievable mess in Victoria. It registered 9.8 on the scale! They've had helicopters swarming over taking pictures!"

She held him apart from her. "We are going to re-build this condominium complex."

"We are?"

"Yes! The bunch of us who own it. We have to re-build. Victoria has to be re-built, and we'll have to do our share."

They moved back up the rock and sat down. "Your neighbours all seem to be down at the Rec Centre. They thought you might be in your garden. I walked here, and then, Thank God! I saw your note."

"I walked home from downtown, and most of that after dark. With no streetlights on."

They discussed all that had happened, and the first business that they had to do.

"When I saw your red field poppies," Trevor finally said, "I thought, you know, of Dad being in the military years ago, and I thought how appropriate; 'In Flanders Fields.' Do you know what I mean?"

Mona put a hand on his back. "Remember the accidents and close calls and scares we've had over the years? Well, your father and I have an Issa haiku we like to recite. 'Just simply alive,/ Both of us. I/ and the poppy.'"

"Mom, Dad is dead!" Trevor spoke sternly, trying to over-ride the break in his voice. "Oh, God!" He said and bawled. "It was so much worse than I expected!"

"I know." Mona spoke calmly though tears stung her eyes. "I was there."

YOU WITH THE CROWN ON YOUR HEAD

*I*t was mid-December, and Alec had a new mistress. He was out late night after night, and at home he tossed and turned and showered all the time.

"Work, work," he muttered. "'Tis the season."

"Play, play," said Kathy, though not aloud.

She knew who it was — a buxom neighbourhood blonde called Kay, about her own age, married, with teenagers still at home, who wore bright red earmuffs to set off her pale mounds of hair. Kathy herself was buxom enough, but her own children had left Quebec, and her hair, still dark brown, was straight as a pin, flyaway fine. She almost welcomed winter as then she could hide it with a hat until spring. Hats kept her head warm too, and she chose them carefully, knits or felts, to last for years, not months. She could see that earmuffs were more fun, also that fun and silliness were in short supply around her house. But at least she had peace and quiet as Alec would be working late, again.

Ten days to Christmas, 16 to the dawn of a new millennium. Decisions should be made, some changes, though she couldn't for the moment think what they might be. And even if the children couldn't get back, tag-ends of shopping always appeared at the last moment, so she decided to go downtown to Ogilvy's in the afternoon, though she was usually better at things in the morning. It was a dark afternoon, too, and she hadn't had much for lunch. The weather was bad and due to get worse, a foot of snow had arrived, and rain was compacting it into bands of gray sponge. The temperature was dropping, and the sponge would freeze into dimpled icy sheets along sidewalks and streets. But she knew what she was doing. If she fell and broke a leg, twisted an ankle, strained her back, she could blame the weather, or politics — not the mistress, leave that unsaid. If nothing happened, she'd wake up sleepily when he came in, and say, "I had such a hard time downtown with all the traffic and crowds; how did you find it?"

She took a bus down Cote des Neiges, transferred at Guy along Sherbrooke to Mountain. It was very dark now, at four o' clock, and the wind was getting colder. Old black hat down over her ears, coat collar up, boots hiding the runs in her stockings. She wouldn't be trying anything on, after all. She hadn't bothered with makeup, the rain would wash it off, just a little lipstick as she'd left, an afterthought. No need to let down completely.

It was nice to be alone; she didn't fuss so much when walking, especially when every footstep had to be plotted. Wreaths hung in some shop windows, lights looped around in others, the effect was cheerful, and it did her good to see it all. Lots of people were out shopping; they passed her burdened by great bags and parcels, as if everything bigger was better. She wasn't sure what she was looking for in Ogilvy's, not a hat, certainly not earmuffs; it was something she'd know when she saw it, nothing fancy or splashy or big.

"*Est-ce que je peux vous aider, madame*?" the sales people would say.

"No thanks, not yet." She'd keep them waiting.

Though it could be anything, apparently. Alec had said so, what had he said? Something ridiculous.

He had said, "There's lots of money now, lots and lots, we can do anything we want. Go downtown and buy yourself a present, why don't you? Anything you want."

"But where...?"

He interrupted, "Stock market, bonds, compound interest. Go out shopping." He said other things she didn't understand; money was like politics, she got the fundamentals, but the details shifted away, out of her head.

"There's nothing I need or want."

"You haven't got anything, really. Wouldn't you like to spruce up a bit? We might even leave Montreal sometime soon. Start again somewhere else."

"Maybe nothing's better than something; maybe it's too late to change."

"Oh, for God's sake, go buy yourself a hat. You like hats."

"If you've got so much you can put it in the poor box, or give it to Centraide."

Spend, spend was an odd line of chat for him, even out of guilt, usually he scrimped as much as she did. Save, save for a rainy day, save, save for snow or sleet. Was there more to that conversation than she'd heard? Stride on down the dreary street, and then let come what may. There was nothing she wanted, but she was going to Ogilvy's anyway. Buy something small and simple, think of something like that to look for, at least.

Wooden clothes pegs, for instance. Wooden clothes pegs with enough spring in them so they'd hold more than a piece of Kleenex. There was a perfectly good clothes drier in the basement that she didn't use, not for his things, or bed linen, anyway. He'd bought it when he was finally sick of having soot from the furnace all over his underwear, wet sheets slapping him from the cobweb of laundry lines down there. Not so subtle on her part, perhaps.

She'd find some clothes pegs and buy some for herself, and some for the church's ongoing used-clothes-line sale on Sundays, basically rummage, but you do what you can. Clothes pegs on hangers held up the rumped-out old skirts that someone might want to try on. She'd rather wear her own things to rags than try to fit into someone else's shape. Hats were different, but people didn't give them away in winter. A Hat For All Seasons, someone had safety-pinned onto the brim of an old fedora, which came down to her nose when she tried it on.

27

Walk a little faster and get off this beaten track. But she couldn't, too many people before and behind kept her linked in line, step sideways and you needed firemen's boots or skates.

Her family back home in the Maritimes had never believed in excess, quite the reverse; they pitied show-offy people who had such meagre inner resources. Her grandfather and her uncle were both Church of England clergymen, one in Charlottetown, the other near Halifax. There was a faint tincture of holiness about her family, holier-than-thou-ness, which they acknowledged in irony, thinking that destroyed it. Which it didn't, quite, she could see that much. And the notion that less is more didn't sit well with the rich anglos of Montreal, not old black hats and runs in your stockings, anyway. But when you've been brought up with church voices in the background, advising virtuous poverty, and you slowly go deaf in different surroundings, there has to be something else to warm your body, your head, your heart. Not that she'd found it.

Her father hadn't taken the cloth — he left PEI, came to Montreal and became a lawyer, and she was proud of him. But guilt made him unduly humble at times, even subservient, he agreed too often. The bite of his comments were felt only at home, especially at meals.

"Have some Tabasco with your mashed potato," he'd say, if someone seemed complacent. "Get some marmalade on that grim blood sausage," if outrage seemed too fulsome. And always jam with cheese, for more balance of sweet and sour: she thought of how horrified, and then amused, Alec's mother had been at that revelation, jam with cheese, like a child's sandwich. Adults had cheese alone with good bread or crackers, with fruit, perhaps, at the end of a meal. There were no surprises at that table.

Her own mother, edgily ambitious, made sure that she understood about table napkins, the placing of knives, forks, and spoons, glasses and plates.

"Make mistakes, and you'll never be asked to Buckingham Palace, never have tea with the Queen."

But she undercut all that information if she thought Kathy — or even Alec, later — was getting uppity in some way.

28

"My-si-my, well, dearie me, look at the crown on your head."

At the corner of Mountain and de Maisonneuve the lights were red, the water deep off the curb. A taxi splashed the front of her coat. Someone pushed a package into the small of her back. Her boots were already soggy, so when the light turned green, on she went.

"Oh, how the red cliffs and the blue bays were lovely on a summer afternoon." Her mother often talked about Prince Edward Island, but never went back, as far as Kathy knew, and never found any new cliffs or bays around the island of Montreal.

"I was rocked in the cradle of Canada, no traffic jams in Charlottetown, no blowing of your own horn either."

She'd been pleased with Alec as a son-in-law, though privately she called him "a mercantile Scot," a step up from farming, but still, someone in trade. Churchmen and lawyers belonged to professions; they didn't buy and sell things. In England they'd be considered a higher order than people in trade.

Lots of other girls wanted Alec; other girls called Kay, mostly, at least two girls called Kay. She'd managed to marry him and had never been sure just why he wanted her, except, of course, she'd sit still for anything, and sit still she had, through blonde mistresses and dark, long hair and short, even through a Kay with red ear muffs, for God's sake. And it wasn't as if he'd had any money. His old people, his mother, his aunts lived on and on, holding the purse strings, and he couldn't find a job that paid well, so she'd been able to go on with the penury of her past, at least. The ironies continued, perhaps she begged them into existence, perhaps she couldn't live without them.

Those girls called Kay went on and married rich young men, had big houses and cleaning women, dressed well, looked pityingly at her when they saw her ongoing little outfits, nothing new again this season, well no. But she didn't have time for clothes, the Kays did no laundry, washing or ironing, no bedmaking, no vacuuming or taking out the garbage, or setting the table, doing dishes, cooking, dealing with children. What on earth did they do all day, lie around fooling with needlepoint?

The one down the street worked quite hard, looked after her children, had an absent husband and too much energy to burn. Anglo husbands had to travel a lot, to make any kind of living. Look at Alec, so often away. No, don't look at Alec.

He gave her the odd little pin, sometimes a bracelet, and if the mistresses were given more, she didn't care. Then, her father, long retired and harkening home, decided she was getting too big for her boots, a little too proud of her place in the world, and needed taking down a peg, so he gave her a garish purple glass pin, costume jewelry from Birks, so she'd be excited by the blue box before she opened it. You with the crown. At least when Alec gave her a blue box from Birks, there was something real inside it.

'For richer, for poorer,' why not for poorer, for richer, the way it usually happened on earth? Because the wedding service was concerned with the riches of heaven. For richer, for poorer, for the real thing, later on. But the 21st century is supposed to be an age of adulthood, heaven arrives on earth in two weeks. Milk and honey will run in the streets in the next millennium, run in great streams on earth and then also in the sky, with any luck. What lies and nonsense, look at the gummy slush on this sidewalk. And even that, and everything else may vanish completely. Charlottetown began the great sweep of the country; Quebec City may turn to dust. There's no heaven at all without solid earth under your feet.

She'd almost reached the side door of Ogilvy's, and thought she might go around the corner onto Ste. Catherine to see the window of moving stuffed animals, but it was now very cold, and the side door so inviting under its canopy, that she turned into the shop. Traditions should be broken, sometimes.

Going through the revolving door, someone bumped her again; people were so careless, and the woman pushed past her, as well. Kathy pushed back, and they emerged into the shop at the same time, into a soft wind of warm perfume, and even if the shop had puffed delicious currents of scent around the doors to tempt people, she blinked with pleasure. Then someone was shaking her hand and wishing her happy holidays, and smiling nervously at her, a face melting with spangled rose colour, pale hair waving gently over the forehead. She might have pushed harder if she'd seen who it was.

"But you haven't been walking in this frightful weather? So damp, and taking away all our Christmas snow? I drove down, well, sort of, there's so much to do these days, isn't there? Must dash; it's the small things that get you in the end, isn't it?"

Kay, without the earmuffs, jittering at her as she sped away. The waves of perfume faded, and the lights at the cosmetic counters, the jewellery displays brightened and enlarged into barricades that fenced her out. Clothes pegs would be unheard of here, unless she asked for one made out of diamonds, then she could clip it onto the edge of her hat.

The afternoon's expedition was over; she'd accomplished her purpose of getting here, having some time off, and now she'd go back through the revolving door, and she'd be fine once she was back in the cold.

But outside Kay's green station wagon stood at the curb, and inside Alec sat in the driver's seat idling the engine; sat idly inside listening to soft music, no doubt, looking out at the wayward mob struggling with new sleet and slush, the white streaks of old salt and black dirt of last year's sand. Skis were sticking out through the back window and, when she got close, she saw an old hockey bag, mitts, ski poles, skates. Her car had looked like that, a few years ago.

She turned away, up to Sherbrooke and the bus stop up there, mindless, unfeeling. No, she'd make a stand; sometimes you had to stamp and stand. She could play mistress perfectly well, if she wanted to, the keeper, not the kept. Circling the rear end of the green car, she stood in the street being splashed. She gestured imperiously, she thought, and rapped to catch Alec's attention, make him roll down the window.

"Your mistress," she said, "your mistress, Kay, I mean, will be out in a minute. When she's finished her shopping."

"Kathy," he said, "this is not the way."

"Not Kathy," she said, "never again. It's Catherine now."

31

No saint, no queen, no crown. What a relief. She glanced wearily at the street sign a few yards away, Ste. Catherine Street. And she'd walk along its shabby lengths in a few minutes to make sure of who and what she was.

Alec folded his arms around the steering wheel and bowed his head.

No repentance, no more guilt, it was too late for that. Anger was better, to force him away.

"Don't block the traffic," she told herself, "and don't show off." But she pulled her hat down firmly and scraped the buckle of her purse hard against the shiny paint of the car's door. And again, long and hard.

His head snapped up, eyes glaring. That's better, she thought.

"I want you and Kay to move away," she said. "A new marriage for a new millennium. Leave me the house and a little money — since you have so much — and just go away. That's what I want."

You could grasp the limits of about a hundred years, and feel your way around some other clusters, here and there. But more than that, centuries flapped and folded like sheets and pillowcases pegged onto endless clotheslines.

The new order would be different for her, as well. She'd use that basement drier, for instance. Alec and Kay would leave for some strange mainland town, and she would stay home in her own island city. Kathy from Charlottetown. Catherine of Montreal.

OLD FRIENDS

he sudden shrill of the telephone at 11:00 p.m. on Tuesday night caught Natalie by surprise. She snatched it from the cradle, wondering who could it be, and what disaster had occurred.

"Natalie Davis, is that you?"

"Yes, this is she, and who is this?"

"How about three guesses?"

If there was one thing Natalie hated, it was strange voices trying to play games on the telephone. The fact that she was in the throes of preparing for bed annoyed her even more.

"If I had a lot of time I'd play the game with you, but I don't, so either you identify yourself or I'll hang up this minute," Natalie snapped.

"*Sic luceat lux*," or how about,

'The quality of mercy is not strain'd;/It droppeth as the gentle rain...?'

She gasped as the wind was knocked out of her. The first three words were her high school motto and the quotation was a verse from Shakespeare's *Merchant of Venice*, which she had performed magnificently in high school — thirty years ago!

"No, it can't be...Joanie? Joanie Sanchez?"

"Surprise, surprise, Natalie Davis; it's still Davis I believe? This is a voice from the past. Remind me not to tangle with you; you are one tough woman," Joanie said, with laughter in her voice.

Natalie burst out laughing. As she recovered from the shock, she stuttered, "How...where...how did you find me? Where are you? How are you?" She couldn't believe it. She just kept throwing questions at Joanie before she could answer them.

"Slow down, kiddo. I can only answer one question at a time. I'm fine and am calling you from Boston," Joanie said.

"Boston, is that where you live?"

"No, no, I live in Jamaica, but I'm on my way to an art exhibition in New York. Mildred, one of my good friends, is an artist, and she lives in Boston. She is exhibiting in a show..."

"When did you get to Boston? Oh, Joanie, I'm so excited." Natalie interjected before Joanie finished. "New York, you are going to New York? When?" By this time, ideas were formulating in Natalie's head.

"Natalie, I'm dying to see you. Sorry, I can't visit you because I don't have a visa for Canada, among other things, but how about if we rendezvous in New York?"

"Just try and stop me. A rendezvous with my long lost, best friend from high school? Oh my God, is this exciting or what? When can we meet?"

"Natalie Davis, you're still crazy. I'll be arriving in New York, Thursday night; I'll be staying at the Sheraton-Manhattan Hotel. Can you meet me there, say Saturday? I know it's not much notice, but I only have until Monday."

"You're on," Natalie said, confident she would be able to arrange it.

"I can't wait to see you and to catch up on all these years," Joanie said.

For the first time since the conversation began, there was silence. It was an awkward silent moment, then Joanie added, "There is one small catch." She paused to get Natalie's reaction.

"Catch, what catch? Joanie, you always loved to dramatize. You haven't changed a bit. What is this all about?"

By now, Natalie was beginning to sense that there may be more to Joanie's phone call than a chance for them to get together.

"Oh don't start playing Miss private detective now, Natalie. The catch is, the art show is billed 'Art into the Millennium', and as the name suggests, it is being held on January 1, 2000."

Natalie sighed with relief. "So what's the big deal?" she asked innocently.

"Well, for starters you may have to travel on New Year's Eve. Are you not afraid of the Millennium bug? Haven't you heard about all the possible accidents that may happen?"

"Oh, now I get it! You think things may be chaotic and I may not make it?" Natalie was back in good spirits.

"Yes, that is my fear. Mildred and I are arriving in New York on the day after tomorrow, December 30, so we won't have that problem. In any event, we have to be there ahead of time to set up our display. But you, when do you think you can arrive?" Joanie sounded sheepish.

"I don't know yet, but I'll contact the airlines and the train depot and get back to you on when and how I'll arrive. Millennium or not, I'll see you in New York!"

"Yes, do that. I'll give you my number right now: 917-243-7889. I really hope we can meet — for more than one reason Natalie; thirty years is too long." She rang off.

Having recovered from the shock of hearing her friend on the phone, Natalie's mind accelerated into overdrive. She visualized Joanie the way she was thirty years ago: petite, just over five feet, cute, with large brown eyes and the most gorgeous mane of glossy black hair hanging over her shoulders. And those legs! Natalie had lost out on many dates because of Joanie's shapely legs. They were bosom buddies all during high school, sharing desks, romance novels and lunches. She saw it as clearly as if it happened yesterday, the Saturday they had gone to the movies to see *Doctor Zhivago*. They had worn their in vogue, psychedelic-coloured tent dresses. Natalie had saved every penny of her lunch money for two whole weeks while they shared Joanie's lunch, just to have enough money for them to go to the movies. At the end of the show, they had hurriedly left the cinema, distancing themselves from the seats they had occupied. It was an embarrassment. Looking back at the peanut shells, grape pips, apple cores and the chocolate wrappings on the floor, one would have thought a couple of pigs had been let loose in the cinema. Oh, the joys of their teenage years! Now they planned to meet again — after thirty years. She couldn't wait. Natalie sighed and her heart began to palpitate.

* * *

At noon, on December 31, Natalie caught the Amtrak Train bound for New York City.

Not being a gambler, she felt if the millennium predictions came true her chances would be slightly better by train versus air travel. She was in for a long, leisurely ride. At the end of the twelve-hour trip, she would witness the dawning of a new Millennium in 'the city that never sleeps'. The train laboured along its rehearsed journey, stopping at many stations along the way. Trying not to think negatively, she wondered how many times the train had done the trip before, and how many accidents had occurred during those trips. Would they make it safely and incident free this trip?

She observed the landscape, beginning with the Canadian countryside. December 1999 had surpassed all records as the warmest experienced in decades. Everywhere, on the hillsides and in the valleys, the grass appeared beige or varying shades of brown dispersed with patches of green. On the slopes, the wind played tag, ruffling blades of grass, as it blew against the grain. Clumps of leafless thickets stood bare and foreboding in some areas, waiting for spring to re-clothe them once more with foliage. Small patches of graffiti had begun to peek out from the sides of buildings, bridges, and large shipping containers. Lord, I hope it will never get to be as bad as New York City, she thought.

Natalie read the magazine she had bought at Union Station for a while, admired the scenery again, then lapsed into reminiscing...Me and Joanie, what a wonderful friendship we had, the secrets we shared, the letters we wrote to each other during our summer holidays, giving blow by blow descriptions of everything we did — those letters were pages of diaries really.

Suddenly, her palms felt clammy and her heartbeat raced. She sat up straight in the high-back seat on the train. What will I look like to Joanie? Will she recognize me? Will she still like me? She dashed to the washroom at the back of the coach that she occupied. She sat on the toilet seat after carefully layering it with tissue, but she couldn't "go." The trick of running the tap always worked at her doctor's office, but it wouldn't work now. She got up and dumped the tissue in the garbage slot. She stared at herself in the washroom mirror above the sink as she washed her hands.

"My face looks pudgy; my eyes are no longer bright and clear as they used to be in the Sixties," she mused aloud. Pulling up her skirt, she looked at her legs, all celluloid and crinkly. She imagined Joanie still had her sleek, smooth legs. She rubbed her index finger over her front teeth — yes, the once even white teeth were now a darker shade of pale, with a gap between the two front ones. Aging is a bitch, but it has been thirty years, she told herself. She stepped back from the mirror. Oh my God, I'm fat. I'm not bloated or flabby, but a tight fifty pounds more than I was the last time I saw Joanie. She placed her right hand on her tummy, pressing on the small mound. Darn it, I should have joined the gym with my girlfriend Connie. Why oh why, didn't I stay on that weight loss program three months ago? I was doing so well. Now I've put back on every ounce I lost. She began to panic, but there was nothing she could do to change her figure or her looks overnight. In less than nine hours, she would be facing her high-school best friend.

At the United States border, the train stopped for almost an hour while immigration officers boarded the train. Two of them entered the car in which Natalie was travelling. They interrogated every passenger, and she eavesdropped on some of the conversations. The officers were questioning Frank, a middle-aged black man in the seat opposite her for the second time. Natalie had struck up a conversation with him earlier, and he had mentioned that she had nice legs. She had blushed bashfully, thinking, 'If only you had seen Joanie's legs, you wouldn't give mine a passing glance.'

"Is Nigeria a part of Africa?" one immigration officer asked Frank.

"Yes, it is sir."

"What do you do in Canada?"

"I'm a systems analyst."

"Any ID?" He produced his ID.

"What kind of job do you do?"

"I'm a systems analyst," Frank replied for the second time.

"What's your address?"

It seemed the immigration officers were not letting up as they tried everything to trip up the poor guy.

It was good therapy to listen in on the conversation for it took her mind off the anxieties she was experiencing. The immigration officers took Frank off the train for further questioning. Natalie was relieved for him when he returned to the train several minutes later. Finally, the train continued its journey to "The Big Apple."

After a while, Natalie couldn't focus on any particular memory anymore, couldn't read anymore. She couldn't see the landscape anymore. The creeping shadows of nightfall had replaced the greyness of winter.

At Penn Station, Joanie was waiting to meet her. Joanie had positioned herself at the top of the escalator, a vantage point which allowed her to see every passenger who came off the train. Natalie ascended the escalator with her weekender in one hand and her tote in the other. She saw Joanie immediately, and took the moving escalator two steps at a time, anxious to greet her friend. Joanie looked straight at Natalie then looked further down to the other passengers ascending the escalator. Joanie didn't recognize her! With a jolt, she awoke from her slumber. The old Indian woman behind her, dressed in a mustard sari, was tapping on her shoulder.

"Do you know what time it is?" the woman asked.

Now, what could be so important on a train that she had to know the time at this precise moment? Natalie willed herself to remain calm, then checked her watch.

"It's seven minutes to midnight," she said.

As she spoke, the urgency of the request dawned on her. Suddenly, there was a lot of activity on the train. The porters hurried from car-to-car, distributing noise makers, passengers stood up to stretch the kinks out of their limbs, while some rushed to the washrooms. Natalie noticed that some passengers had retrieved Bibles from their luggage. She whispered a quiet prayer. The Millennium Bug is real; she prayed that it wouldn't affect the train. In the midst of the bustle, the driver announced that there would be a ten-second countdown.

Everyone returned to their seats, and the driver's distinctive voice crackled through the microphone; ten, nine, eight...Like a well rehearsed chorus, the passengers echoed his words, seven, six, five...you could slice the tension with a knife, three, two, one, z-e-r-o!

Pow! A loud explosion rocked the train. 'Oh my God, it has happened! Is this the end that the pundits had predicted?' she thought. With bated breath, the passengers waited. Soon, like a tidal wave, relief engulfed the train. The porters had uncorked several bottles of champagne simultaneously. They began handing out little plastic glasses of the bubbly, and the passengers greeted each other with "Happy New Year!" Natalie felt the tension dissipate as everyone realized that the dreaded hour had come and gone. All the doom and gloom of the past year were over — at least they hoped so.

At Penn Station, Natalie was one of the first passengers to alight from the train. She practically ran up the stairs of the moving escalator. Looking around on either side of the stairs, she spotted Joanie instantly. Still petite, smile still wide and white, hair now slightly grey, hung over her shoulders. She dashed toward Joanie. Then it hit her like a bullet between the eyes. Natalie dropped her bag, and her mouth gaped. Tears spurted from her eyes. The tears blurred her vision for a moment as she gazed at her long time best friend. Joanie didn't move; she didn't stand up to greet her friend — she couldn't. Natalie observed that Joanie was harnessed to a wheel chair. A closer look revealed the awful truth, Joanie had no legs. Mildred, her friend, came forward and picked up the bag. Taking Natalie by the shoulder, Mildred consoled her.

"She didn't know how to tell you all these years," she said.

A HEARSE OF A DIFFERENT COLOUR

s our bus turned in to the public parking lot beside Claudia's Restaurant, the lights glared full upon a tall man with a sign he was holding up toward us:

ARE YOU READY ? For Y2K ? BE SAVED

The fog seemed to magnify the light beams, and the man was more in our face than he imagined. He was wearing a white cloth wrap, like a toga. He twirled the sign's stick and the other side read:

YEAR 2000. Be SAVED. Join in the RAPTURE.

The air brakes made that whistling sound like letting off steam, and we glided to a stop in a gravelled area beside the fog-shrouded restaurant. I slung my backpack over one shoulder and, carrying my laptop, got off with the driver. He hauled my suitcase out from the locker under the body and dropped it at my feet.

"You carrying lead around, boy?"

"Books," I answered. "Just a few books." I'd been wondering if I should tip him but he solved that easy enough.

Cub Reporter Arrives in Bayberry. Settles Hash of Upstart Bus Drivers.

I picked up the heavy suitcase. It had my thesaurus and dictionary and a couple of my favourite novels with the space around them filled in with clothing. There was a sign over a side door saying Restaurant and Bus Depot. Thought I'd better go in and make some inquiries. Maybe have a bite of supper.

"Going someplace in particular?" The voice seemed to be directed at me. I turned a bit and there was this old geezer with his head stuck out the window of a long, white automobile.

Now, I'm not one to mind a question or so, but this was pretty abrupt. I'm thinking, 'Who wants to know?' But, being polite I said, "Why do you ask?"

"Well," he said, "I do the taxiing 'round here, and this here's my limousine."

Reporter Greeted on Arrival by Limo. Expects to Soon Unravel the Local Cult Scene.

"That's good," I said. "I usually like the exercise of walking and carrying my bags, but this one's a mite heavy, and I'm not sure where I'm going."

"You don't know where you're going?"

"I've got to find a boarding place. Nothing fancy, you know, but I'll be staying awhile. Like to stay with ordinary people."

"The common people?" The old geezer was looking me up and down, and I wondered if he noticed my pants were a couple inches short of high fashion. The battered old suitcase, with my father's monogram on it, was no fashion statement either. It spoke of money in a very negative way. The old trench coat slung over my arm was also a hand me down, but that might not be so noticeable.

"You know any good places?" I asked.

"Hemlock Hotel might be good. They usually have a room out the back where they can put a boarder. You could talk to Mrs. Meisner."

Geezer's walrus mustache was bobbing up and down as he spoke. It was brown tobacco-stained along the bottom.

"But I've got to have a bite to eat first."

"I'll join you. Time I had a cup of coffee."

The old fellow knew everybody, nodding and speaking to people as we went into the restaurant and found a booth. We sat down, and he stuck his hand out toward me.

"Walter Honnicutt," he said. "Taxi driver, mortician and limo service."

"James Hawkins," I said. "Reporter."

"Same name as our editor. You must be related."

"George is my Uncle," I said. "I'm here to help him out for a bit."

New Reporter Reveals he has Media Connections.

"Wasn't aware he was short of help."

"Temporary," I said. "More if I get a break."

A fulsome blonde waitress came over to us. She was a real looker, sort of a filled out Meg Ryan. "Fancy meeting you here," she said to Walter, laying out water, fresh place mats, and a menu.

"My daughter," said Walter. "Honey, meet James Hawkins. New reporter."

We acknowledged each other. We made our orders, and she bustled away.

"Who was that fellow nearly got run down by the bus?" I asked.

"Oh, him. Langley Meisner. Watch out for him. Claims to be an ordained minister. Don't know where he got it. Also claims to be an accountant. Has an Investment Management Service. He has $4,000 of mine I can't seem to pry loose. Said he could make it grow. Tell you, I think he made it disappear."

"What was that sign about? Y2K Rapture?"

"Oh, he says the second coming is near at hand. Join him and be taken up to Heaven in the Rapture. Year 2000."

43

Honey arrived with our orders. "Don't you talk like that," she said to her father. "You know he's honest, and he'll lead us into the Rapture, too."

"He's crazy. Keep away from him, I'm telling you."

Domestic Quarrel in Restaurant Divides Small Town.

We finished at the restaurant and went back out to the parking lot where Walter's long white vehicle waited in lonely splendour.

"Throw your bags in the back and hop in front," said Walter.

I opened the back door, and there was no back seat — just a clean flat floor stretching back to a station wagon style rear. I lifted the suitcase in, tossed the backpack on top and settled myself into the front seat.

Looking around I said, "This isn't your ordinary taxi."

"No siree. Any time you're getting married or anything special, you want a limousine, just give us a call. We fit the back seat in and Bob's your uncle."

"George," I said.

"George, I meant." He looked at me kinda funny.

"So you must have a hearse, too," I said.

"Yes, of course."

"But this isn't it," I say. "It's white."

"Who says a hearse has to be black?"

"I do," I say.

Reporter Uncovers Shady Practices of Morticians.

"O.K." said Walter. "You make judgement on my mortuary practice, and I'll make judgement on your stories. I hope George is easier on you than I'll be."

At the Hemlock Hotel, Walter grabbed my backpack and left me to lug in my suitcase. I asked him to wait with me while I spoke with Mrs. Meisner.

As we entered the door, Walter Honnicutt took the initiative, yelling out, "Lucy, got a customer for you."

"Well, maybe," I said.

Lucy came from a room down the hall. She was short and wide and waddled. I wasn't surprised when her speech reminded me of quacking — a sharp blat followed by a receding burble.

She showed the room over the back ell-peaked ceiling and a big window at the end. There was a single bed, a dresser, a small table and a closet. Washroom down the hall. "Electric heating, your own meter." There was an ominous tone to Lucy Meisner's voice.

But the weather was warm enough. What did I care about electric heating bills. Wouldn't take much for my reading and for my laptop computer.

We agreed to a month's rental in advance. I figured I might want to move on — or not.

"Let me get you a donut, Walter, before you go. You too, Mr. Hawkins. Just stop in the parlour there." She walked away down the hall, burbling happily. While we waited, in came a gangling young man, who made me think of Ichabod Crane.

"Mrs. Meisner's son," said Walter, introducing the beanstalk, whose height contradicted his maternal lineage. "Langley Meisner. No doubt he'll try to sell you something."

"James Hawkins," I volunteered. "Reporter."

Young Meisner was dressed in a grey suit. He wore a clerical collar, and on his lapel was a large yellow button with the words: Are you saved? He didn't react to Walter's remark.

"You're selling religion?" I asked.

Mrs. Meisner came in, carrying a tray with donuts, a teapot, cups, and started dispensing.

Walter took a donut, said, "Business calls," and was out the door.

I sat on an old grapeback sofa and parked my tea and donut on a side table. Across from me, there was a large, framed print by Jack Gray of a fishing vessel. Langley paced the floor, ducking each time he passed the hanging glass light.

"No, I don't sell religion," he said. "I promote it. I encourage it, but I don't sell it. Avocation only."

"Hmm," I answered, non-committal.

"What I sell is financial advice. That's my business. Mutual funds, stocks, money markets. You want to get your financial house in order, come and see me."

Well-heeled Journalist Banks on Knowledge of Local Investment Guru.

"You work from home?" I asked.

"No, no. I have an office downtown. You'll see it. Zenith. A couple places down from the News."

The next morning the rising sun was right in my window. Looking directly out to the eastward, I could see a spruce and grass covered headland. To the right of it was the little harbour, mainly of use to the local fishermen, and to the right of that, a point with a small automated lighthouse.

Below my window, at the end of the driveway, there was a camper trailer. On the side of it, beside the doorstep there was a bumper sticker saying: If this rig is rockin', keep on walkin'. Seemed like Langley was something of a braggart.

As agreed with Mrs. Meisner, I had breakfast in the Hemlock's dining room, along with Langley, a travelling salesman and a young couple from Ontario who were 'back home' visiting the birthplaces of their parents.

It was a ten minute walk down to the News. I arrived there about 8:30.

"We got some funny rules 'round here," said Uncle George. Quite a big man, hands like hams. He wore a Boston Red Sox baseball cap while seated behind his overflowing desk. Didn't strike me as much the intellectual. "What we do here, we stay as late as we like. We can come in early as we like, but if it's after 8 a.m., you're late. Get it?"

"Yes sir," I said.

Breaking News: Workers Trampled by Media Management.

"Another thing," Uncle George leaned back and folded his fat hands behind his head. He was on a roll. "You might think reporting news is the big thing 'round here. Wrong-O. Advertising is our life blood. So what you're going to do is pay your way with some ad sales."

Media Mogul Blackmails Minions.

"Doesn't sound too bad," I lied.

"I'm going to start you with obituaries. Old Stan Greeno has just died. No close family. You'll go up to the Oaklawn Home and talk to them, and then over to see Walter Honnicutt. Get the details needed. Now here's the crunch: you take ad samples to these people, and you sell them. I'll help you get them ready."

Uncle George took most of the morning showing me around, all the time painting a bleak picture of the newspaper business, and the worse he pictured it, the more excited I got about it. We mocked up a couple of sample ads on the light table.

"These are only jump-off pieces," admonished Uncle George. "Let the clients tell you what they want."

"I don't think I'm much of a salesperson, Uncle George."

"Oh yes, you are. You've been attentive and polite and asked questions. You'll do fine. You've already persuaded me to take you out to lunch and to give you a week's advance pay."

We jaywalked across the street to Claudia's. She greeted customers with a wide smile and a cheery comment as she bustled between the counter, the kitchen and the cash register. We found an empty booth, Uncle George sitting on the side facing Main Street, giving me the view of some harbour and the fish plant across the parking lot next door.

There was a perky little brunette serving at the front booths, and Walter Honnicutt's winsome daughter waiting at our end.

"Hi, Honey," said Uncle George.

"Hiya, Mr. Hawkins." She had a smile for me too, looking me over pretty appraisingly, but I got the impression I was too young for secondary consideration. She left menus and water with us.

"Walter's daughter," said Uncle George. "She's back from a few years out West. Calgary, I believe. Boys 'round here call her Honeypot. She does part-time, the busy hours — noon and suppertime."

Uncle George took the seafood chowder, and I took the fish and chips. Haddock. Some good, you! Claudia sure knew how to do up that seafood. And the coconut cream pie wasn't bad either.

After lunch, I made my way up to the Oaklawn Home and got the vital statistics on Stan Greeno. They said he was an ordinary guy. No close relatives. Maybe a niece in British Columbia. They were trying to make contact.

I cut across on Church Street, past the Anglican, the Baptist, and the United Churches, all in a row, all overlooking the sea from their perches on the hillside; down Hill Street to the Honnicutt place. There was the old house and the old barn that, in its day, had stabled horses for the coach that used to run along the shore road, joining the coastal communities. Now there was a newer building close to the road. It was neatly painted white with black trim. Over the right-hand side was a sign saying W. A. Honnicutt Mortuary.

The left side was a double garage. The doors were open, and the space was empty. I knocked on the Mortuary door. No answer. I wandered into the empty garage. There were two doors toward the back. At the right, there was a carpentry shop containing a coffin partly built, on two sawhorses. The back door led to a stable and beyond that a corral where I could see a nice looking palomino horse. I turned back toward the big open garage doors, and Walter was just returning from some mission. He stopped in the street and backed his long, white limo-hearse into the garage.

"Hiya, James," he said. "You've come for a visit?"

"It's official," I said. "I'm doing the obituary on Mr. Greeno."

48

Walter climbed out of his cab and went to the back, opened it up and dragged out a bale of hay. "Grab that bag of oats, will you?"

I obliged and we manhandled the two items into the stable. The bale of hay was left on the floor, but the oats had to be secured in a metal box.

"Official, you said. Come into the Mortuary, and we'll talk business."

I followed him into the other part of the building. There was the body of an old man in a coffin. He appeared to be sleeping.

"Stan Greeno," said Walter. "Doesn't he look regal?"

"What was he like?" I asked.

"Quiet. He never bothered anybody. Played outfield for the Seahorses when he was young. He was a dory fisherman on the Lucy M. back when WWII started. German sub came up, ordered the men to take to their dories, and sank the vessel with gunfire. That annoyed him. He went and joined the merchant navy and had his ship sunk by a torpedo. Those merchant seamen never got any recognition. He just worked in the fish the rest of his life."

"Thanks," I said. "I ought to be able to use some of that in the obit." I pulled out the ad Uncle George had helped me construct. "What do you think about placing an ad with us?"

"George is getting some mileage out of you, eh? Here, let me see." Walter scrutinized the little ad, running his finger down the list. "Taxi Service, Limo Service, Mortuary Service. You didn't mention anything about hauling hay and feed."

"We could put that in."

"No, don't bother. You can run it, as is."

Move over, Conrad Black. Make room, Ken Thomson. Intrepid Newsman Carving New Niche.

Hustling around for the News, I got to know the town and its people a lot better, but some of the same characters I had noted on arrival became more and more prominent. Claudia, I got to know on a first name basis. She knew more about what went on than Uncle George. Honey usually waited on me and always wore her welcoming smile. She only worked the noon and supper shifts, so she had some free time in the mornings and afternoons. Sometimes I'd see her riding her palomino on the beach or the path to High Head.

I went into the Zenith Investment Advisors office and sold an ad to Langley Meisner, but when I proudly showed it to Uncle George, he just said, "We'll print that when we're paid for the last one."

On Saturday night, I sat in Claudia's and as I ate, watched a spectacle develop out in the parking lot. There was Langley Meisner out there, wrapped in a white sheet, strumming a guitar and singing. There were a few people gathered around.

Honey came by with my coconut cream pie. "Isn't it wonderful?" she asked.

"Good pie," I said. "Best of kind."

"No, you," she said. "The Y2K. Rapture. The Second Coming. I'll be there." She leaned close over me and whispered. "I hope you'll be there, too."

Prominent Reporter offered Inside Track to Heaven.

"Where is all this taking place?"

"So far, we're planning on High Head. We practice going there."

"When's the big event?"

"Early in the Millennium. We don't have an exact time."

"Is this supposed to be 2000 years following Christ's birth?"

"Ayeh."

"As I understand it, our calendar is off a couple of years."

"That's the thing, it could be any time now. You sound such a Doubting Thomas you'd better check us out. I'll be getting out there as soon as you finish your pie."

Sure enough, I'd no sooner joined the little group of audience when Honey appeared at Langley's side. She had a sheet wrapped 'round her and a tambourine in hand. She joined right in, and their harmonizing was sweet as they sang "When the roll is called up yonder, I'll be there."

"Will you join us on our trek to High Head tonight?" asked Langley.

"Mind if I take pictures?"

"Not at all. The world needs to know about this."

"I'll get my camera and follow."

I stopped at the News for my camera and following along Main Street, turned on High Road, past the Hemlock Hotel. Streetlights ended, and I could see the frenetic flashlights of the little group in front of me as we made our way up the path to High Head.

They stopped at the height overlooking the cliffs and, after a prayer, got into another hymn. I moved up and took a few flash shots while they sang. I expected good pictures — the subjects didn't flinch, they weren't exactly camera shy, and they were wrapped in those white outfits with a black sky behind them. Great contrast.

Local Photo-journalist Produces Greatest Photos Since Karsh.

Next morning there was another death, and by mid-afternoon, I was on my way over to see Walter Honnicutt. He'd been at his after-lunch session of checkers at the fire hall and I met him walking part way along the street.

"How's business?" I asked.

"Brisk, James, brisk."

"I hear there's been a death at the wharf."

"Yes. Eden MacIsaac. He's resting at my place. I can give you some details. You might want to check with the police and coroner as well as the family on this one."

The big garage doors were open and the long, white vehicle was in its usual place, facing outward. But the machine was rocking.

"He's not at rest yet!" I said.

"He's not in the hearse," said Walter. "He's in the mortuary."

We both approached the vehicle. There were voices.

51

"How's that, Honeypot?" a voice like Langley's. "Yes, yes, yes!" a voice like Honey's.

We peered in the windows. Two bodies thrashing around. Clearly, it was Honey and Langley.

Walter thumped his fist on the top of the car and yelled, "Get out of there, you hellions." Then he turned and ran for his office. I just stood and watched.

The back doors of the hearse flew open, and Langley clambered out like a spider in flight. While he headed toward the front door, Honey was clawing on a T-shirt and scrambling for the door to the stable.

Walter came flying out the office door waving a shotgun. For a moment he hesitated, then pointed the gun toward the ceiling and fired, first one barrel and then the other. Both miscreants were now out of sight.

Walter turned to me. "What can you do?"

"Just a case of Rapture," I said. "Getting ahead of the game. There ought to be a story in this."

Journalist Reveals Meaning of the Rapture. Nobel Prize Nomination.

ECLIPSE

Hanu was born with a hare-lip and a cleft palate. It was all his mother's fault. Everyone in the village had warned Madhu that a pregnant woman who handles a cutting instrument during an eclipse runs the risk of having a deformed child.

But Madhu hadn't listened. "*Arre!*" she had muttered, as a shadow seeped across the sun, suffusing the afternoon with a dun-coloured light. "If I stop now, who will feed my children?" And she had continued cropping grass, squatting on her haunches and inching forward swollen-bellied and crab-like, working the small curved blade close to ground. When the sun emerged three hours later, it lay close to the horizon and the contractor-*sahib* handed Madhu twenty rupees — her full day's wages.

As the baby emerged from Madhu onto a thin reed mat, the village midwife, who was also her aunt, said, "So it's a boy this time." But there was a constraint in her voice that made Madhu peer closely at the baby. He was crying — a snuffling mewl — unlike the defiant yells of her daughters when they had issued forth from her.

The child had a wizened monkey face, with coarse black hair growing low on his forehead, eyes close-set and small under overhanging brows. And his upper lip was open to the base of his nose, his gums bloodied, as he laboured and snorted mucus from his flattened nostrils.

Madhu took the baby in her arms. "I will bathe and oil-massage him myself," she said to her aunt. "You can go now."

Her aunt sniffed. "Yes, yes I'm going. Who would want to stay? Such a stubborn ignorant woman you are! See what your twenty rupees has brought you!"

The baby opened his eyes and looked up at his mother. And in that instant, between the infant's rictus-contorted scrutiny and his mother's answering smile, there grew a fusion as ancient and mysterious as the dance of the earth, the sun and the moon.

"Come," Madhu said, "come drink, my little Hanuman, my little monkey-god," and she thrust her nipple into his crippled mouth, coaxing her unnaturally swollen flesh between his exposed gums. "See," she added as her milk flowed responsive and urgent, "for you my son, I've brought forth *doodh* so fast-fast."

The village was small, and the news of Madhu's son spread quickly. If Madhu was aware of the glances of pity or derision thrown her way, she gave no sign of it. She continued to take her place as usual in the line up at the village well each morning. Filling her earthenware pots and carrying them home perched against her hip, she did not linger to gossip. "Shameless woman!" The women would whisper as she walked away, her back erect. "Thinks she's better than everyone else in spite of that monkey son of hers!"

Despite village expectations that the child would die within a few weeks, Hanuman thrived. Wrapped tightly in a thin cotton sheet, Madhu would take him with her each morning. Lying placidly on a mat as his mother cropped grass, he would smile crookedly when she paused to croon to him. By the time he was a year old, he had grown sturdier and taller than other children his age.

As the seasons wheeled through the village, bringing famine one year and floods another, the talk about Madhu and her son died down. In between these calamities, there were periods when village life resumed its placid flow, its surface occasionally broken by small items of news which rose like flotsam, swirled briefly in a froth of gossip and then sank out of sight: Jhunoo, the daughter of the village silver-smith had been affianced to the son of a wealthy gold-smith in a faraway town, and it was rumoured that her dowry had been over a hundred thousand rupees; Ramji, the fruit-seller who sat by the railway station gates, died and his widow had to be restrained from throwing herself onto her husband's funeral pyre; Beena the wife of the Mission school washerman had given birth to a club-footed daughter. It was whispered that though the mid-wife had sensibly offered to smother the child, Madhu, who was present at the time, had slapped her aunt across the face and threatened to report her to the police.

In the summer, when the earth lay fissured under a sky of burnished steel, Madhu stayed home. While her daughters swept the floor of the hut or scrubbed utensils, Madhu would sit by her son, cleaning rice. She would pick out a small stone from the grain and lay it by Hanuman. "*Ek*," she'd say, pointing and holding up one finger, and when the next one was laid next to it, she'd add "*Do*" and then "*Teen*" as the third tiny pebble appeared. At two years of age, Hanuman was talking, his pronunciation mangled, but the words understandable. By the time he was three, he could count to fifty. At four, he could repeat the stories his mother would tell him as she chopped vegetables or fanned the flame of the small *chula* on which she cooked their meals. Sometimes, to test whether she was listening, he'd add his own embellishments and his mother would laugh, give his shoulder a push and say, "Hanu, *hut-ja*! I never said that!"

When Hanuman was five years old, Madhu decided it was time he went to the Mission school. It was free, and her son would learn to read and write English. His father, sitting on his string *charpoy* under the *neem* tree that grew beside their hut, hawked a stream of betel nut juice into the dust. "What for?" he asked "What will he learn there? Fancy writing, that's all! To give him big-big ideas. To make him think he is better than us, his *ma-bap*. No, next year he will come with me and learn how to load and unload *samaan* onto the trains and lorries for the contractor-*sahib*. Start earning some money."

"Or better he joins Gemini circus," snickered his eldest sister, "as a performing monkey."

"Yes," said Hanu, "like this...see." And he gibbered, leaping onto the *neem* tree and swinging from the lowest branch. His father laughed, and his youngest sister clapped her hands and giggled.

"Stop it, you stupid, good-for-nothing boy!" His mother caught the end of his tattered shirt and pulled him down. *"Besharam! Ooloo!"* she hissed and clouted him across the side of his head.

"Arre, ma!" he protested, "How can I be a fine monkey and a shameless owl at the same time?" Such impudence would have earned his sisters another slap, but his mother ignored him and went back to kneading a ball of *aata* and rolling out *rotis* for the family's supper.

Later Madhu said to her husband, "Well alright then, he will work with you in the afternoons. But in the mornings he will go to school."

Hanuman may have been named after the great mythological king of the monkeys in the epic tale of the *Mahabharata*, but to his school-mates he was *"bandar-bachha"* — a monkey-child.

*"Naatch karo bandar, paisa mille ga!"** The chant would follow him onto the playground. And he would caper and mewl, and screw his face into monkey grimaces, playing to his audience with self-parodying gestures and four-footed leaps across the yard.

"Why do I have to go to school, Ma?" he whined.

"Because I say so!" she snapped. Then she added, "Do you want to become a coolie like your father? Pulling hand-carts, carrying loads on your head in the hot sun, till the veins in your neck and your legs turn into thick ropes, and your brain becomes like a bale of straw? And you smell of coal-dust and gunny-jute?" She caught him by the shoulders. "Not for you, Hanu. You will learn to read and write. And maybe the Mission will pay for your studies all the way to matriculation, just like they did for Janaki's son. Someday you too can become a big-big *babu-sahib*, sitting in a nice office with an air-conditioner in the window, and wearing a white shirt and officer-pants with soft *chappals* on your feet."

(*Monkey do your dance, and you'll earn a little cash.)

By the time Hanu was fourteen, the teasing in school had stopped. The children had grown accustomed to him. Some were even a little afraid, for he was a strange one. He could read and write — even in English — better than anyone else. And he did calculations in his head that made the teacher frown in puzzlement. He was also amazingly strong and nimble. Once, when he was only ten, in response to a taunt, he'd scaled the topmost branches of the huge *pipul* tree in the school yard in a trice. Dangling by one arm, thirty feet or more above his audience, he'd yowled and scratched his armpit. His tormentor and the small crowd of children that had gathered to watch, backed away. He'd swung down, flashing his misshapen grin. "*Arre! arre!* What happened to you all? Don't worry I won't bite!"

There were no more gibes after that.

Except from club-footed Neela who was two years younger than Hanu. "Did your mother use a knife during an eclipse, too?" Hanu had once asked her. She had tossed a glossy plait over her shoulder and shot him a withering look. "No Hanu. God made me like this only to show off His skill at making cripples. He's even cleverer than you!"

Hanu took to sitting under a tree, waiting for her each morning on his way to school. He could see her approaching from a distance, hips swaying sideways as she swung her deformed limb forward. A dip, a pause, and then another drunken lurch. At first, he had fallen silently into step beside her but she had limped on, indifferent. On the third day, he turned cartwheels and somersaults on the road. He walked on his hands, waving his legs in the air, knotted his legs around his neck and rolled like football head over heels till his hair was spiky and talcumed with dust.

She glanced at him. "I heard that one of Lalloo's performing monkeys died last week. Why don't you go work for him?" she said. "He'll take you from village to village, and you'll become famous dancing to his *dholak*."

He hung his head. "I just want to be your friend, Neela."

Neela was silent for a moment. Then she shrugged. "Well, alright then. But stop behaving like this. I don't need a fool for a friend."

57

"You just don't like to see me do what you can't!" he jeered.

She turned on him, snarling. "Yes, and I don't like to hear your *billi-miaowing* either. Go away. Now!" To his astonishment, she was crying.

"Please Neela," his words tumbled out thick and garbled. "Please, I'm sorry, sorry, sorry." He stopped in front of her. "Here, slap me on my face, on my head, anywhere." He caught at her hand. She wrung it free and hobbled past him, stony-eyed.

The next day, she relented. Hanu was so pleased he almost did a cartwheel, but stopped himself in time.

Sometimes, Neela was accompanied by a girlfriend and Hanu would either vault over a low wall that ran by the side of the road before they saw him, or wait until after they had gone some way ahead before continuing. It would not be seemly for Neela to be seen walking with him.

* * *

When Neela turned fifteen, her parents decided that she no longer needed to go to school. It was time to find a suitable match for her. Her father, a washerman employed by the Mission school and hospital, had let her attend primary school — even though she was only a girl — because it was free and because he'd hoped that this would reduce the cost of her dowry.

"I'll marry you," Hanu said. "No dowry, no nothing!"

"But you haven't asked whether I'll marry you, *bander-bachha*," Neela said.

Hanu growled. "Don't call me that!" He turned to her. "Neela, I'll get a good job. Last week Mr. Mathur — remember him, our math and science teacher — said he would recommend me for a job in Bombay when I complete my matriculation exams next March. His brother is a big-shot director-*sahib* in a pharmaceutical company. They want someone to help their laboratory research department." He added, his voice nasal in his eagerness. "It will be a new life for us, Neela. Away from the village. Meeting new people. Maybe a small place for us to live — just you and me together."

Neela looked at him. At eighteen, despite his disfigurement, he was not unattractive. His brown eyes, under shaggy brows, were expressive, and his black hair fell in curly waves across his forehead, giving him the slightly rakish look of a Hindi film *"heero"*. He had grown tall and muscular, and moved with a lithe grace.

"And a fine pair we'd make!" She said. "A cripple and a monkey-man — *Shrimati lengra-tengra* and *Shri bandar-mantar!*"

Hanu spread his hands. "Neela, that's silly"

"It isn't silly, Hanu. We are deformed. Ugly. People will look at us and laugh, or turn away in embarrassment."

"What does it matter what other people think or say, Neela? Why are you always looking through everyone else's eyes? It's what we feel inside that matters. That," he tapped his temple, "and what's up here. Brains! That's what's important."

"Maybe. But you'd have to be blind and deaf, to ignore other people's opinions Hanu. Or very stupid."

Hanu interrupted. "Okay, okay. Perhaps you are right, perhaps I am right. It doesn't matter." Greatly daring, he touched her hand lightly. "Neela, I don't care what anyone else thinks. All I want is you to be my wife." He wheedled. "Besides, Bombay is a big, busy city. Who is going to find time to laugh at my hare-lip or notice your foot?"

She looked at him for a long moment before answering. "All right Hanu, I'll marry you. But I must go now. It's getting late."

Hanu leaned against the crumbling wall of the Quila. He and Neela had been meeting secretly by the ruins of the old fort, for more than a year — ever since she'd left school. He smiled thinking of the first time they'd met there in the gathering dusk. The Quila was supposed to be haunted, which was why the villagers shunned it. Neela had been more frightened of the *churail-bhoot* who was said to live in the banyan tree next to the wall of the Quila, than what would happen if they were discovered.

"That's all nonsense Neela." Hanu had said. "I've been there many-many times — even late at night, and the only *bhoot* is the wind which sounds like it's crying when it blows through the broken walls." He'd pulled back his shirt sleeve and flexed his muscles. "See this? No *churail* is going to hurt you, don't worry."

Looking at the old fort it was easy to understand its reputation. It stood at a bend in the river, its mildewed ramparts jutting like rotting teeth through tangled grass and thick creepers, home to a colony of bats and the occasional jackal.

They would sit watching the river in the brief tropical twilight, sometimes skimming flat stones over its surface, or playing a game with pebbles on the back of their hands which had to be tossed up and caught before they fell to the ground. Neela would tell him about the latest movie she'd seen on the TV that belonged to the village headman, Nathu Ram. Sometimes she'd sing some of the songs too, as the story unfolded.

He'd shown her an exercise book with stamps stuck to its pages. Some of them were from England and the United States torn off envelopes addressed to the Mission and given to Hanu by the office clerk.

Most of the time Hanu listened, not talking much himself, to the rise and fall of Neela's voice, and her laugh which sounded like the low gurgle of pigeons. When she smiled, her teeth were as small and white as grains of sago. Sometimes she was grave, worried about her father's rheumatism, aggravated by standing in the river, washing clothes day after day. Occasionally, she would pass on some small tidbit of village gossip, giggling through a small hand cupped over her mouth.

In all this time, he had not so much as touched her hand until tonight. What it would be like, he wondered, to feel the flutter of her hands on his face, to let his mouth linger over the soft swell of her breasts, to cup his palms very gently over the knobby stump of her club-foot and to feel her body shaped to his own hard strength. He shivered in the warm night air.

Madhu was sweeping the courtyard in front of their hut after their morning meal. When Hanu began to talk, her *jharoo* stopped moving, and her face went very still.

"So many changes, so soon," she said. "Going away to the big city. And, your father, he'll grumble about not getting a dowry." She shook the *jharoo* to release a small cloud of dust. "But I think it will be a good thing. What does it matter if Neela limps a little. She will make you a fine wife." She bent again to her sweeping, thrusting the *jharoo* in short, hard strokes against the beaten earth. Without looking up, she added, "Well, don't just stand there grinning like a fool. Why aren't you at the station helping your father? The train will be here any minute now."

* * *

The village lay on a main railroad route, but while most freight and passenger trains flew past the small station, the Bombay-Delhi Express halted for three minutes each day, disgorging villagers and their belongings. The platform, usually deserted except for crows and a few goats, would be galvanized into a melee of passengers, hawkers, coolies and beggars.

Hanu sometimes dreamed about what it would be like to travel on the Express. To look out of the window as the station platform slid away, and his village disappeared, and the next village came and went and the one after that, till they all blurred into each other, and the rush and speed of the train filled his nostrils, his ears, his brain. The horizon would stretch far, far beyond the rim of the world. And other lives would press about him like an intoxication. Something like his stamps which, with their foreign designs and postmarks, conjured up vistas of strange and wondrous places.

He was late. The train had already arrived. Pushing a baggage trolley in front of him, Hanu worked his way through the surge of passengers and hawkers. Up ahead, a family of foreigners — a burly man, his wife and a little girl with blonde curls — were standing on the platform, and Hanu caught sight of his father unloading the last of their baggage off the train. "Where have you been?" He asked sourly, as Hanu began hoisting the bags into place on the trolley. The Bombay-Delhi Express jerked into movement and began to pull out of the station as a freight train whistled its approach to the opposite side of the platform.

What happened next, happened very fast. But also with horrifying slowness. One moment, the little girl stood near Hanu's baggage trolley; the next, she was gone. As the crowd pushed past her, heading to the exit gates, Hanu saw the child teeter, and then tumble over the edge of the platform. The freight train loomed enormous at the far end of the station. For an instant, Hanu stood paralyzed. Then thrusting his trolley aside, he hit the rails, swooped her up and leapt back on the platform in a single, smooth movement. The freight train locomotive, shrieking hysterically, pumped past them. The child, too dazed to cry, looked up at him. He set her down, dusting her dress off carefully. Afterwards, he couldn't recall doing that. All he remembered was that he'd staggered away, leaned over and vomited onto the rails.

* * *

A week later, Hanu lay on an operating table in the Mission hospital. When he floated back up into consciousness, his upper lip was a staircase of small stitches and his palate hurt when his tongue rested against it.

"It will take a little time to heal," the surgeon said to him. "But six months from now there'll only be a hairline scar. You'll be better than new." He punched Hanu's shoulder gently. "And hey, just wait'n'see how the girls go for you then!"

"So lucky for me that Harrison-sahib was visiting the Mission hospital," Hanu said to Neela and his mother. "He's a *burra* surgeon-*sahib*. Famous. He can charge big-big fees. But for me — free!"

"Lucky for you? Hah! More lucky for him! Their daughter would have been *chutney-masala* if you hadn't been there," Neela said.

"Well, anyway...now you'll have a handsome husband, instead of a *bandar*," he rejoined, laughing.

Neela didn't reply. "Shall I help you cut onions, Maji?" she asked Madhu who was preparing the evening meal.

Three months later, Mr. Mathur had good news for Hanu. He had been in correspondence with his brother in Bombay. Hanu would have to go there for an interview after his exams were over. "My brother says that if you are as intelligent as I said you were, then the job is as good as yours," Mr. Mathur said, beaming. "The pay isn't much to start with, but the opportunities for advancement are excellent."

"So, I will go there and work for a year, and save some money," he said to Neela, articulating in his unfamiliar new voice. "And then I will come home for our wedding, and you can come back with me to Bombay."

Neela said nothing. Hanu noticed that of late she no longer teased him, or laughed as readily at his antics. Something between them had tilted out of balance. "What is it?" He asked her finally. "You've changed Neela. Are you unhappy?"

She was silent for a long time, fidgeting with the hem of her sari. She said, "I'm not going to marry you Hanu." Looking up at his shocked face, she added, "No, wait. Wait. Don't interrupt. Listen to me. You are right — you are no *bandar-bachha* anymore. But I — I am still a cripple. People will look at you with pity and wonder why you married me when you could have had a pretty young wife. And perhaps a nice dowry, too. And you will start to look at me differently. And I will start to look at myself differently, too."

He opened his mouth to protest, and she cupped her hand tightly over his lips. "No! Listen to me Hanu. I haven't finished. You will be ashamed of me in Bombay. And I will be humiliated by your shame. Not at first maybe, but after a little while." She took her hand away and added, "I cannot — I will not — sacrifice my pride. Not even for you." She swallowed hard and looked down.

"Neela, I don't want anyone else except you. I will never, never want anyone else but you. I don't care about your foot, I don't care about anything like that...Neela, please, Neela..."

But she was gone. Hanu touched the scar tissue above his lip. It would fade in time. To a fine thread, barely noticeable.

It had grown dark. Somewhere far beyond the Quila, a jackal yowled — an eerie, yearning cry. He looked up at the full moon, and watched a shadow curve across its surface. He sat there unmoving, and slowly, slowly the moon became sickle-thin and sharp as a grass-cutter's blade.

NOTHING CHANGES

The tree is ancient, and the old man sleeps under it. He mostly sleeps there in the afternoon, and sometimes even in the evening when the heat is unbearable. Morning naps are rare. But today, he can feel things starting out different. His limbs are heavy, his heart weak; his mind hazy. He has to close his eyes.

Right away he dreams. His dreams are always subtle; terrain and landscapes of the two greener seasons, floating by...and the gentler people that populate his life. Sometimes the stable animals, too, the cows and the donkey, the sheep. He never dreams his wife.

Though sometimes when he's coming out of his dreams, but still hanging in the lull of sleep, he can see her at the window, watching him. Then he purposely keeps his eyes closed for a while longer, hoping she will go back into the inner part of the house...for mostly seeing her there is not just a dream, but something like a sixth sense, pupils of the mind.

"Old man," he now suddenly hears her shout. "What are you doing? It's only ten o'clock, and you're sleeping already. Come and start the fire! I have to get the food to the people in the field — have you forgotten?"

Carrying a bundle of kindling in his arms, he tries to pull himself up the stairs to the second floor of the house, for the stables are down below. He doesn't feel the pain in his back, not the way one feels a fresh pain. How many years has it been part of him? How many years...and how much more can nature curve his body...and how well nature has taken care of not breaking him in two, but mould and mould him to its own desired shape and twisted ending....

"Beat the eggs," she says, furious with him. "Beat! I can't be late! Not on a day like today, when you don't need to rub a match to make a flame. The world will burn with a sun like this.... Besides, they're late cutting the wheat — they're trying to hurry to catch up."

He picks up a fork and sits down with the bowl on his lap, starts mixing the heavy yolks. He has no strength in his arms, but it's only an omelet she's making, not a cake. The eggs mostly need to be blended.

"Whip!" she says. "What are you afraid of?"

His hand slows down. "What day is it today?"

She doesn't answer for a long time. But after she has flipped the omelet onto a plate, she pauses for a moment to straighten herself and rest. "You will see," she says to him. "You will see."

He watches her as she puts things into the wicker container: tablecloth, forks, a dishcloth; all the food she has prepared for the customary midmorning breakfast. Her breathing is heavy. Although younger by seven years, she too is old. What would he do if she died? Somehow God better be kind and settle him into a grave first.

She refuses to take the donkey, but carries the basket on her head, the way she has done for years. Only now he worries about her tripping on a stone or getting her foot caught in a stray vine as she makes her way downhill along footpaths and furrows.

"What day is it?" he asks again as she puts the load on her head, and straightens herself for the journey.

"Count," she says. "For once, count...."

Even in anger, she keeps her balance.

A tear sits at the corner of his eye. He can feel it there, like a soft bead. If he'll leave it alone, it'll remain there...and then when he's not thinking about it, it'll spread and dissolve, barely moistening his thin, thin lashes.

The sun is already a fireball in the sky, and it's not even noon yet. When she reaches the wheat field, she's ready to collapse but is careful not to show it. Her daughter-in-law comes to meet her and takes the load from her head. She carries it under the tree, where the others are already sitting, waiting.

The tree is skimpy, but it's the only one there. A frail covering of shade is better than no shade at all. There's no source of water nearby, not a spring nor a river, where they can go and cool themselves. She has brought them a jug of water, but they'll need that to wash down the dust from their throats...and take some of their thirst away. Nobody asks what day it is. Not like that fool up at the house.

An automobile is heard coming along the valley road. All morning only a truck has passed by on its way to the next town. They all know it's too early...but eyes turn anyway. They all watch Letizia....

"The sickle," says Letizia's husband, suddenly jumping up. "It's dull. Christ, can't we have some sharp sickles for once?"

"Sit down and eat, Amedeo, before the food is gone," says the son. "I sharpened the sickles last night. I did them all. Nothing wrong with your sickle."

Letizia brings her hand to her temple, touches a strand of hair that has come out from underneath her kerchief. She doesn't tuck it back in, but twists and rolls it, winding it tight like a thread.

"I'll show you how to sharpen a sickle," says Amedeo, wiping sheets of sweat from his forehead. The anger on his neck is turning purple.

"I'll take the bloody thing to my house and show you. I'll show everyone!"

"Amedeo," warns the other man, a neighbour. "Where are you going? Nothing changes. Too sharp a blade is no good. Think of fingers missing from your hands...blood that doesn't need to be shed...."

But Amedeo can't be stopped. He's already hurrying across the field, the sickle like a wild banner in his hand.

67

"Let him go," says the son. "Let him go. We've done all we can. Maybe it's better this way."

Letizia gets up from the ground. She takes her kerchief off her head, wipes her neck with it, the perspiration down in her breasts.

She will not speak. She never does.

"He'll come back," says the daughter-in-law. "Amedeo will come back."

"Yes," says the other woman, the neighbour's wife. "He'll cool off from the cold water in the house."

"Yes, you will see," says the daughter-in-law.

Letizia lifts her head and slowly starts walking along the edge of the field. Her head is bare now, and her hair is slowly spreading across her shoulders. She ties her kerchief around her waist...and swings her long, flared skirt back and forth, brushing it past her legs. The last they see is the way she kicks her shoes off, and throws them in the ditch.

The neighbour's wife looks around at all the others. "Did you see that? Did you see the way she was acting...and she was singing...did you hear how she was singing...."

"Shut up," says the daughter-in-law. "It's time we minded our own business. Maybe she's doing it for all of us. Maybe she's doing it for Amedeo, too. After all, how can a sharecropper's wife turn down a landlord?"

"A kick in the balls," says the neighbour's wife, but her words are barely a whisper — she's not convinced.

"Talk...talk. We're all good for talk. But do you remember what happened in the other town...when five families were taken away from the land? They had to go back south to the mountains and scrape a living from rocks. This is good land...and the houses are like mansions, compared to what we used to have. We could all be replaced with the snap of a finger."

The two men are very silent. They have dark clouds in their eyes; it's hard to read their minds.

The old lady gathers the forks, folds the tablecloth. "I'll take Letizia's place in the fields. This work has to be done."

"You'll do no such thing," snaps the son. "And don't argue. That's all we need on a day like today, to have to pick you up from the ground...and who do you think is going to run to go get the doctor, with the world burning up...."

"Yes, do as you're told," says the daughter-in-law. "Letizia will be back tomorrow...Amedeo, too."

At home the old lady tries to sleep, but her eyes just won't close. She can't even rest on a chair; she can't sit still. She feels the pumping of her own heart....

Going to the window, she opens the shutters. Slowly begins to undo her bun, loosening the long thin strands of gray hair. She picks up the honey-coloured comb from the windowsill, and holds it in her hand...watches the old man sleeping under the big tree. She wonders what it would be like to put her hand on his forehead, to touch him once more before one of them is going to die....

The old man is dreaming. He's dreaming a river shaped like a sickle. A small river, where thatched, sunburned grass is cooling into the water, along the edges. But is it a dream, for he knows he's not quite asleep yet...? It's really more like an image, a flicker of familiar landscape and terrain...and an old woman at the window, getting ready to call his name....

ONLY IN PASSING

*S*ome reunion," said Aunt Olive, her one good eye glaring in my direction. I smirked and tried turning away but that wavering eye caught me. "I don't want to be here," Aunt Olive grumped in her throat, sounding like she might hork. Her agitated fingers, thick and knobby, clutched at the air.

"Come around to the front of the cottage," said my dad's wife Millie, taking Aunt Olive by the arm. "This is your trip down memory lane. Remember when you lived here?"

Aunt Olive yanked her arm away and glared at the crooked veranda. Three other vehicles from our convoy manoeuvred into the lot by the cottage. My relatives spilled out onto the sand.

Millie ran to scoop up her four-year-old and cooed into Lisa's blond curls. They joined together like a mother and daughter look-alike ad. I felt rage as I watched Millie hugging and fussing over her kid.

A long trip in a car with my dad and his wife is not for me. Even a short trip with my dad and Millie is no fun. Throw in Aunt Olive and my sucky sister Lisa for totally gruesome. Seeing Millie hug and kiss Lisa made me want to spit. I'm nearly ten years older but even when I was Lisa's age, they never showered kisses and hugs on me. When I was little, and Mom was around, Dad used to talk about spoiling kids. Now even he hugs and kisses Lisa and lets her get away with stuff I would have been hung for.

Everyone stood beside Aunt Olive looking out at Lake Huron. The waves thundered toward us, making me feel fierce. I wanted to run up and down the empty Inverhuron shore. I wanted to escape our nomadic family reunion.

I raced down the beach, past the 'Dangerous Undertow' sign and all the way to where rocks piled high and water dashed up. After awhile, I trailed back to the cottage. Dad was pointing to the roof and telling Millie, "Granddad put on that roof."

"Really," she said fascinated. How could a roof be fascinating?

The cottage looked like a four-room shack settling in sand, but my wandering family were thrilled that the owners let us visit for the day. This place meant nothing to me. I had never been here before.

"This is great," said Millie in that peppy way she had. "A walk down memory lane should perk Aunt Olive up."

Aunt Olive was on a lawn chair set up in the sand. She didn't look all that perky slapping at sand fleas attacking her ankles. She sat in a dress with her legs spread wide and her flabby thighs exposed. If I sat like that in a dress, I would be told to put my knees together. Aunt Olive didn't look like she enjoyed memory lane.

I was about to say this when Dad gazed at me with a soft squishy look on his face. I wondered what world he was in. "Connect with your roots," Dad said trying to pull me to him for a hug. I was too big for hugging. I pulled away.

My loud and obnoxious cousins raced in and out of the water, poking sticks in the sand. They were so immature. If they were in my school, I would avoid them like the plague. But here, I had no choice. It was either hang around with them or listen to stories about the roof, the past and the dead relatives.

"Vanessa." Dad interrupted my thoughts. "Take Lisa down the beach for a walk."

Lisa gave me a big smile and took my hand. I hated to admit that

Lisa really was cute and friendly. I wished I could be like her, pretty and sweet and liking everybody. Since turning thirteen, I couldn't seem to like anybody nor could anybody like me.

Dad was watching me, expecting my usual protest. He had this narrow tight look to his face. I surprised him. "C'mon," I said to Lisa. "We'll go exploring, without the others." She looked up at me with big eyes the colour of the lake. We took off our shoes and started toward the dunes.

"God, she's so cute," I heard my dad say, and I knew he wasn't talking about me. He had called me "moody" right in front of everyone when we stopped at Listowel to look at some ugly house where Uncle-somebody used to live.

I carried Lisa piggyback across the stream, and we strolled along the sand toward the dunes.

"Where's Mom?" said Lisa.

"Back there. See the pink lawn chairs in front of that cottage. Want to go back and sit with them?"

"No. I want to 'plore with you."

Just my luck. She wanted to be with me. "How do you like this reunion so far? Sucks, eh?"

"Yeah, sucks."

"Ha," I laughed as we reached the top of the dunes. "They won't like you learning bad words from me. Better not say that in front of your mom." The breeze rippled our shirts, and it felt great. Kind of free and wild. Suddenly I felt happy to be staying here for the afternoon. I just needed to get rid of Lisa.

I saw some guys walking along a far path with fishing rods. Maybe I could meet guys and tell the girls back home. Then this reunion might have something worth talking about.

"C'mon." I walked with Lisa toward the boys, but they disappeared behind some bushes. I heard a clomping noise and saw a rider on horseback trot over a curved wooden bridge. Lisa and I followed. Our footsteps sounded hollow as we crossed the arched and weathered planks.

"It's the troll bridge," I said to Lisa, and I lifted her up to look over the edge at the river below. "This is where old Aunt Olive used to live." The stream wasn't deep, but was green as a lagoon. You could see willowy plants waving like mermaid hair.

"I scared," said Lisa.

She pulled me back toward the roaring sound of the waves. We followed a sand-covered boardwalk. Below us, Millie and the aunts were dancing in mincing steps along the water's edge. Lisa ran to her mom. I galloped back along the shore where their recent footsteps were being washed away.

When I reached my cousin Izzy balancing on a log, I stopped. He smirked at me.

Using a deep ominous voice, he said, "Bones are buried around here. I heard them talking about a burial ground."

"Who cares about old bones?" I shrugged and splashed past him. Back at the cottage, Dad was talking to his brother Raymond and the new wife Bubbles who laughed loudly. Aunt Olive was listening with a grumpy look on her face, her mouth turned down and everything droopy, her chin, her long-hairy eyebrows and even the bright pink ball cap stuck on her head.

"We're like a travelling caravan," said Dad. "Trying to catch up to the past."

"Remember Grampa, always one step ahead of the Sheriff," said Aunt Olive's daughter, digging into a cooler for cans of pop.

"That's probably why they journeyed here in the first place," said Uncle Raymond.

"Why else would you come down the Saugeen on a raft? You had to be some kind of adventurer, desperate or poor. Maybe our family was looking for religious freedom."

Everyone laughed. We never went to church. Any of us.

"How did Grampa ever make a living here? Must have been hand-to-mouth," said Aunt Edith handing everyone a can of pop.

"Lumbering and fishing. Inverhuron had a natural harbour." Uncle Raymond liked to explain things. "Then when the pier burned, people buzzed off to Saskatchewan."

"Not everyone," said Dad. "Didn't you go to a school around here, Aunt Olive? Do you remember?" Aunt Olive didn't reply. The adults exchanged looks. I knew they wanted to buzz off, too. They began talking about finding the old schoolhouse.

Dad looked at me for a few minutes and then said, "Vanessa, stay here, make sure Aunt Olive keeps her hat on. Her skin burns easily. We're going to wander off for a bit."

I made a face. Just my luck, having to look after the ancient one. My dad, uncle and aunts sauntered away pointing at weeds and shore birds. Then I looked at Aunt Olive plump as a cream puff. "What do you think, Aunt Olive?" I said for no reason, not really expecting any answer.

"Sucks," said Aunt Olive.

"Doesn't it just," I said, and we made eye contact. She had this beady and wicked glint in her right eye. The left eye wandered off somewhere in its own cataract cloud.

"The undertow sucks. Sucks you right out."

"Yeah?" I was looking at her, and she was looking ahead at the lake, but somehow I felt she was looking behind at the past, or at some bad dream coming back to haunt her or even ahead to some premonition.

I couldn't help shivering. Probably because a cool mist was moving in and obscuring everybody else but us. I couldn't see the water. I could only hear it.

I couldn't see my cousins, but I heard them whooping. Seagulls screamed a reply. When the sky, water and sand disappeared in the mist, I heard better.

"Got any secrets, Aunt Olive?"

"Nothing I want to tell you, girl."

I felt slapped. "Fine. Do you think I care?" Let her report me for impertinence.

"I had a sister," said Aunt Olive. "I was like you."

"Yeah," I said, not prepared to utter any more words. What did she mean I was like you? I certainly didn't want to think of myself as being like her.

She glared at me with that one searching eyeball and said, "My mother died in childbirth. That's what happened to women then. They hemorrhaged and died. Often happened. Makes you think twice about getting in the bushes with some guy."

She turned her evil eye on me as if she had read the thoughts I entertained in the dunes when the guys with their fishing rods walked by. Somehow, she had this gross ability to make me feel she knew more about me than I did. She was like a warning bell.

"So?" I said rudely.

She ignored my attitude and was silent for awhile. Then she started talking almost to herself. "My father married again after my mother died. Everyone acted like my stepmother was my real mother but she wasn't. She had her own children. All boys. Until finally she got a daughter. Pretty like your little sister."

"Did you like her?" I asked.

"Who?" said Aunt Olive.

I shrugged. "I don't know. Your sister? Your stepmother?"

"We didn't express our feelings then," Aunt Olive said harshly. "Children were to be seen and not heard. You kept feelings to yourself."

"Okay. Fine." Didn't seem like times changed much. I was always being criticised for having attitude and mouth. Aunt Olive was loaded with attitude. Her pores were large. Her skin looked like oatmeal left on the stove too long. She was so gross she was actually interesting.

I thought about describing her to my friends. I could tell them she said she went with boys in the bushes. Had a hemorrhage and her child drowned in blood. My friends would scream in horror.

Aunt Olive started speaking softly. "Her name was Daisy."

"Who was Daisy?" I asked.

"My sister."

Another dead relative.

"Daisy died here."

"Here? At Inverhuron?"

Aunt Olive only nodded, ever so slightly.

"Do people know that?" All the talk about the roof, the raft and the schoolhouse but I never heard anyone mention Olive's sister. Did they know about Daisy dying?

"There's an undertow here," said Aunt Olive. "I was supposed to be watching Daisy. And I did watch. I watched the sand suck at her feet. I watched her lose her balance. I watched as we lost her."

I sat up straight in my lawn chair seeing fingers of mist swirl around our heads. "I've got to live with that my whole life long," said Aunt Olive.

Even though she was sitting next to me, she began to dissolve into the atmosphere. I had a scary feeling go through me. I didn't like the feeling. I didn't want to lose real people. I wanted everyone to come back to me.

My cousins came back making ghost sounds. "Where is everybody?"

"Whooo."

"Over here." I called out, and my voice trembled.

They loomed out at us making monster faces. Then Millie and Lisa appeared. "Getting cold. Hug me, Vanessa," said Lisa, and she threw herself at me.

All bones and soft skin, she balanced on my lap. I could feel her heart beat next to mine.

Then Dad and the rest showed up. "Fog's coming in. Ready to move on to the next point of interest?"

"I'm ready," said Aunt Olive standing up on her tree trunk legs. "Let's get out of here."

"I think she likes going down memory lane," said Millie.

"Tara's next," said Dad. "It's inland. Away from the fog."

"I want to go home, home to Tara," said my uncle in a false voice. Everyone laughed.

"Grampa and family didn't stay here long anyway," said Aunt Edith. "Inverhuron was only in passing."

"Only in passing," said Aunt Olive.

We gathered up our lawn chairs, sprinkled out the rest of the drinks from the aluminium cans and started back toward the vehicles.

"Do you think your Aunt Olive is happy with this little reunion?" asked Millie.

"Oh, sure," said Dad. "She gets to reconnect with her past."

"I think she's getting confused," said Millie. "Some of the things she says are so fanciful. She said you are related to a Queen of France."

"You didn't know of this French connection?" said Dad waggling his eyebrows at Millie.

I hate when they acted mushy, I thought. Next thing you know, they'd be kissing in the bushes.

"Izzy says old bones are buried here," I said hoping to break their attention with each other.

Dad shrugged. "Who knows. So many stories and tales."

"And lies," interjected Izzy who was lurking around, campaigning to travel in Dad's car.

"Some of it's true," said Dad. "Some is true."

"I think Vanessa needs a break from boys," said Millie giving me a half-smile like she was my secret friend. "Vanessa, shall we make this an all-girl car?"

The whole clan was talking at once and moving as a mob back to their caravans. Edith tried directing everyone to different vehicles, but Millie managed to get her way. We were in an all-girl car, Uncle Raymond's shiny big Caddy. Bubbles got in the front with Millie. I had no trouble picturing Bubbles in the bushes.

"This way we have conversations with everyone," Millie said taking the wheel. "We can do some bonding."

I ended up sitting next to Aunt Olive in the back seat. Lisa scrambled in to cuddle next to me. I looked at Aunt Olive encased in her mounds of flesh, drooping down her face like melting fat. Her eyes were hard currants buried in dough. On her mouth gleamed a slash of colour. The magenta stain bled into the lines around her lips. I wondered, when did she apply the lipstick? It was the in-colour my friends used, but on her, well, she looked like a corpse.

Aunt Olive reached out to touch my sister's smooth bare leg. Lisa glanced at the hand, shivered and recoiled from the fingers touching her. Lisa bonded close to me, hot and sticky, like a pint-sized twin stuck to my side.

I looked over to see a tear run its crooked way down Aunt Olive's ancient cheek and dry up at the purple bank of her mouth. Her wrinkled hand flopped about lost in the air. Something made me reach for it. I held it in mine. It was rough and cold, but lightweight, as light as my little sister leaning into my shoulder.

SPACE

*I*n Devon Park, there stands a very old elm tree, protected by a shoulder-high wrought-iron fence with no gate. The grasses and flowers inside the railings form a little island of natural wildness around the tree's huge trunk, offering considerable contrast to the rest of the Park's clipped grass plots and wide pavements. On the fence is a metal plaque with lettering in high relief.

In memory of

MISHA THE PAINTER

whose work has enriched
all the people of this earth and beyond.

2177 – 2224
Vita brevis, ars longa.

This is the story of how Misha became a painter.

* * *

In the year 2200, the urban conglomerate of Edmongary filled only a quarter of Alberta. Misha was 23 then. He lived in Calmar district on the seventeenth floor of one of the prefab high-rises which loomed over the streets of that district, as they did by then in all but the wealthiest areas. He worked in a Calmar café. Pretty low pay, but Misha figured he was lucky. He had a job. That meant, while of course he shared the one large room of his apartment with six others, he didn't have to share a bed. When he came home tired from work and pushing his way along the crowded streets and found his apartment mates had invited friends in, he could stretch out on his bed without bumping another human body. The noise was still there, as always, but Misha could mostly tune it out.

Sometimes as Misha listened to the hype and throb of the mus-ads constantly playing in his café or heard another daredriver roar from the Devon track, he would wonder what it would be like to live somewhere where there were no people. What would silence sound like? What would it be like to be able to walk through Devon Park quickly, swinging his arms full-length without worrying about hitting someone? "Hey," he would remind himself, "at least you can see space here." Then he would pick his way to his favourite tree and stand for a long time looking up at its branches.

It was an elm tree, one of very few left in Canada, so Misha had heard. What had saved it from the disease and deadly people pressure that had wiped out most of the urban forests? Misha didn't know, but every time he saw this tree, he was grateful it existed. He loved its strength and grace, and the elegant curves of its branches reaching up to spread delicate leaves against the sky. Sometimes right before leaving, he would permit himself to touch its bark. Anywhere he could reach was worn shiny from the touches of all the people like him, but even if it didn't feel rough like the bark he could see high up, he could still feel the strength of the tree in his hand. It was worth coming to the park just for that.

But on September 10 when Misha came to visit his tree, he found a horror. Someone had carved big initials right through the bark at eye level. A L + S A , and as if that weren't enough, there was a wide heart chiselled around them.

Love! Misha pressed his hands to his mouth so he didn't cry out. Where is the love in that? How could his tree withstand these brutal cuts, gouged deep into its living wood? Now the ice of the coming winter would penetrate to its old heart and kill it at last, this wonder that had flourished here for more than two centuries. Misha knew his tree was going to die.

Misha lifted up his eyes to the flame-coloured leaves flickering against the cerulean sky. Usually their dance drew him into a quiet space, soothing his everyday vexations and frets. Today though, he was sure the leaves were twisting in pain.

His eyes dropped again to the abomination on its trunk. A L + S A. Damn them, whoever they were! And their stupid love affair, just another of the endless couplings that produced still more people to crowd out what little remained of non-human life. He hated people.

Misha reached out to comfort his injured tree but at the last moment drew back his hand. No, he mustn't stress it further. Instead, he stooped to touch the ground above its roots. An orange leaf dropped close by. He picked it up and held it carefully as he plodded back to the ziptrain station.

How was he going to get along without his tree? He'd thought it was safe to love something so long-lived. All he'd asked was to look at its beauty. He'd barely allowed himself to touch it. Yet now it was going to die too, just like Waif and Yolanne and his mom. His love was like a blight — anything or anyone it settled on withered. Well, he wasn't going to watch the process, grieving and helpless to do anything. Not this time. He would not visit his tree again.

When Misha got back to his apartment he found a party in progress, with music thumping and the raucous laughter of people high on Pleazie pills. He pushed his way to his bed and lay down, still holding his leaf. Pain beat through him, and the noise pounded at him. He clenched his teeth against his rage. He couldn't stand any more.

Misha looked at his leaf. So fragile. He'd better put it away. He rolled off his bed and pulled the album Yolanne had given him from its box underneath. It was she who'd taught him the challenge and delight of collage. He painstakingly placed his leaf on his most recent page, then traced its outline with his fingertip. His tree's final benediction.

Misha had to crawl partly under the bed to put the album away, and as he did so he realized it was quieter under here. The mattress and springs over his head, the thick quilt hanging over the sides, the boxes of his possessions at the bed's foot deadened some of the racket from the room. It was pleasantly dim here too, and he couldn't see the Pleazie-drugged people letting loose. He crawled farther under the bed and lay curled on the floor. It felt wonderful to be so hidden, so private. It was cramped, though. Perhaps he could shift these boxes enough to stretch out his legs. He worked energetically and achieved a long narrow space entirely surrounded by box walls except for a gap where he could enter and exit.

Misha lay there in semi-darkness feeling his midriff unknot and his limbs loosen. Letting go like that meant there was no barrier now to stop his tears. They filled his eyes and welled over in rivulets across his temples and down into his ears and hair. He cried for all his losses. His mom, dying after a long illness three days before his fifteenth birthday. Yolanne, his very own miracle, blossoming after those barren desperate years when he'd had no one, but, like a blossom, dying too soon. Waif. Stupid even to try to keep a dog when he couldn't have him in his apartment, but Waif had been such good company. And now his tree. Killed. All its elegance, its graceful strength, its restfulness — wantonly destroyed. Misha cried and cried for his tree.

Eventually his tears ran out. Misha felt empty, loose, like a popped blister. No one had seen him cry. He smiled wryly. That was one good thing from this awful day. He'd found a refuge. There was peace in that. He crawled carefully out of his hidey-hole and under the covers of his bed. It felt sweetly soft after the hard floor. He'd sleep now.

Over the next months, Misha spent more and more time at home under his bed. He lay for hours in almost-quiet semi-darkness, gazing idly at the beige cardboard walls and the grey cloth cover of his bedsprings. He didn't think about much. It was easier not to. His apartment mates tried talking to him at first, but when he responded minimally they shrugged their shoulders and left him alone. "Too bad he's so down," he heard one of them say, "but if he won't talk, what can we do? Weird how he's always under his bed though."

Misha did not sleep in his hidey-hole. The luxurious softness of his mattress and the warmth of the quilt round him as he snuggled into his yielding pillow were the biggest pleasures left to him in his increasingly featureless life — the butter on his mashed potato existence. He savoured going to bed.

In contrast to his home life, Misha's work became nightmarish. It took so much energy to fight the crowds to get there, to ignore the constant blat of the mus-ads enough to take people's orders. His boss got impatient, having to remind him too often, "You've got to talk. These guys can get the cheap synthe-food I sell at any café on any block. What brings them here is the friendly atmosphere. Chat, Misha. Take an interest." So Misha forced out empty pleasantries, but each day he was more frantic to get home. Once inside his refuge, it took a long time for his body to stop trembling. Only because he knew it was his job which provided him with his bed and hence his hidey-hole did he keep doggedly at it.

By midwinter, Misha's life had acquired a relentless rhythm: the torment of work, soothing grey monotony, the pleasure of his bed, torment again.

Who knows how long he might have gone on this way, but one night, as Misha crawled out of his refuge, his attention was caught by light streaming through the uncurtained window. A full moon, huge and silver, shone down at him. Misha stood dazzled. He lifted his hand to its beauty, but of course he couldn't touch it. The pang that gave him vanished when he thought, "Nor can anyone else." He looked at the moon for a long time. Though it was very late by the time he left the window, he felt no urgency for sleep. He was already rested in a way he hadn't been for months.

The next night as he watched the moon, he realized he wanted to go there. He wanted to touch the moon. If he could feel its reality, maybe he could love it like his tree. His dead tree. Pain cut through him, but he summoned his new strength and wrenched his mind back to the moon. The moon had both otherness and beauty. Its regular waxing and waning was a little like his tree's response to the seasons. Yes, if he could just touch the moon with his own living hand, it might be enough for him. Could he get there?

The next day, Misha voluntarily initiated three conversations. He asked his boss, a customer, and one of his apartment mates about travelling to the moon. Their answers were discouraging but not hopeless. Tourists could visit Selene City, the one large human settlement on the moon, but such trips were prohibitively expensive. Selenites charged exorbitant prices to make a good profit on top of the huge costs of transporting and supporting tourists. Yes, Misha could go to the moon, but it would cost him a full year's wages.

Misha decided to go. It would take a very long time, but touch the moon he would — no matter what it cost.

He began at once. He decided to court the café customers. The effort involved was dreadfully taxing, but he won extra tips and the praise of his boss. After three assiduous weeks, he asked for and got more hours. Three months later, when, despite nearly double the hours and only the most grudging expenditures, his savings were still growing too slowly, he sublet his bed, renting out the top only for daytime use. Misha endured all this by concentrating fiercely on his purpose.

On May 3, 2201, Misha walked into the office of the Selene Select Tour Company and paid his passage. He was booked onto Hecate Shuttle. He made arrangements with his boss for three weeks' holiday and gave his tenant notice for May 24. It took two days to get to Nevada Base, another two for medical checks and simulator briefing. On May 9, he left Earth.

Misha's journey to the moon passed in a daze. The sardine-can conditions of the shuttle were very trying. Selene Select packed in as many tourists as they could, counting on constant entertainment to distract their clients from the discomforts of being so crowded. Misha refused organized games, virtual vids and Pleazies. He spent most of the three-day trip with his back to his fellow travellers staring out a window at his longed-for destination. When he couldn't stand any more, he retreated to his hammock. But even there, he couldn't escape his extreme anxiety just to get there, to touch the moon at long last. When, finally, he climbed into his seat in the lunar lander which was to take them from the orbiting Hecate to the moon's surface, Misha was trembling so violently he couldn't do up his own straps.

But Misha's first steps on the moon did not bring him release and satisfaction. The lander's airlock opened into an echoing docking hall. Its passengers were shepherded across into the spaceport offices. Misha still was not touching the moon itself — this was just a human building. Misha followed the Sel Sel serviceperson numbly past various officials who handed out schedules, food coupons, and regulations, issued him a change of clothes to replace the ones he'd been given just before leaving Earth, then directed him to one of several waiting vehicles. Hummers, they called them — small, roofless, electrically powered. "When we get outside," he thought, and his hands clenched on the stuff he'd been given.

But they didn't go outside. The hummer rolled through malls, in and out of huge halls, up and down ramps, until it stopped outside his chosen accommodation, a single bed in a dormitory run by the Sel Sel Service Facility. Misha dumped his clothes and crumpled papers on his bed and looked around. Apart from a holo labelled Tycho Crater on one wall, it was standard hostel. Had he ever left Earth?

That question reverberated in Misha's head throughout the next few days. Life in Selene City was all inside. Living quarters, work space, shopping arcades, recreation facilities, Pleazie parlours, eateries — all were part of the one enormous multilevel complex that was Selene City, and all were just like such places on Earth. Just as crowded too: the moon had lots of unused space, but it cost too much to maintain more than was absolutely necessary.

The only way out of the city was on the Sel Sel Out of the Dome!

Tours. Since there were none of these scheduled till Day 4, Misha took the various tours to examine the physical workings of the domed city. He visited oxygen-producing algae plantations, hydroponic gardens, the water reclaiming plant, the solar power station. The ingenuity of these and the thrift of their production left Misha marvelling at humans' resourcefulness and ability to wrench any environment to their own service. But this too he had seen on Earth.

One difference Misha did notice immediately and constantly was the difference in gravity. He liked the soaring feeling when he jumped, but his constant overbalancing and jerking to correct miscalculated movements made him feel alien in his own body. Rather insubstantial too. Not easy.

Then at last it was Day 4. Misha stood inside his hectic lime spacesuit in an exit hall, waiting while the Sel Sel people made one last inspection. Voices jabbered in his earphones. Sheesh, they'd said all this six times already. Could they not just go? What? Yes! He pushed to the front as they entered the airlock.

Misha was the first one out when the lock door opened. He took three clumsy jumps far ahead of the guide and away from the waiting transport crawler before dropping to his knees to lay his hand on the moon. And he felt — glove. Tough smooth cloth padded with insulation. He still was not touching the moon. He never would. He could not put his living hand unprotected on the bare surface of the moon.

He cried out and hunched right over, rocking a little in his terrible disillusionment. He was unaware of the guide's repeated questions in his earphones, barely felt the hands lifting him up by his elbows, walking him back inside the lock, stripping off his spacesuit. He pulled himself together enough to nod yes, he wanted transport back to his dorm, but once in the hummer he asked the driver to stop at the first Pleazie parlour. He couldn't handle this devastating disappointment without help.

Nevertheless, he was back with the tour group outside the dome each successive day. If he could not really touch the moon, he could walk over her uncovered surface. At least the moonscape was alien, and the harsh sunlight unfiltered by anything but his helmet mask was unlike the soft yellow light which reached Earth. He could see vast distances. If he chose carefully where he looked, he saw no vestige of human life. Was that possible?

There was no other life either, he eventually noticed. There was dust and rock in various sizes and shapes. There was not even wind here to give the illusion of life by blowing the dust about. Without wind to drive eroding dust particles, the edges of all the rocks were sharp, stark — uncompromising in the pitiless stare of the sun. Dead. It was all dead. A sterile desert endlessly hostile to any life. And colourless. Black. White. Inky shadow and blinding glare. He could see for miles, but what he saw was right outside human experience. People were irrelevant here. The only way they could deal with this landscape was to deny it, hide it with buildings, pretend they were still on Earth.

Misha found these tours increasingly unsettling. It was a relief to climb back into the crawler and sit beside fellow human beings. The garish Day-Glo colours of their spacesuits fed his colour-starved eyes.

Misha spent his last two days on a trip spaceside to Artemis Dome, the huge observatory built way back in the first days of colonization on the side of the moon never visible from earth. It was fulldark there those two days, ideal for observing. Misha found his first ever look through a telescope fascinating, but what he was to remember all his life was sitting on an Artemis roof with just the transparent dome between him and the stars.

Here was quantity undreamed of. There must be more stars than there were people on Earth. Even if he limited himself to the big ones and looked narrowly in one direction, he could not begin to count them or even estimate their numbers. There was a new infinity everywhere he looked. Misha felt tiny and utterly insignificant, a mere molecule amid countless worlds of complex creation.

Here was variety. Size, brightness, colour. Every variation surely. Could a human eye appreciate that much change? Awed, bewildered, Misha strained to discern and name the differences. He couldn't stop struggling to order what he saw, but his struggles made him feel incapable, impossibly limited.

Here was space. An immensity beyond conception, a vastness threatening to engulf him. Misha clung to the edge of his bench, dizzy at the perceived threat of spinning off into nothingness.

And here was beauty. Astounding. Heart-stopping. The pure essence of beauty. He could not qualify this — there was no imaginable improvement. Misha was whirled into it, gasping his wonder, frantic at his inability to respond adequately.

Misha got into trouble with the tour guide because he had to be fetched from the roof after a search which considerably delayed the return flight of their jumpjet to Selene City. Deaf to the radio announcements broadcast throughout the complex and on the roofs, he'd had to be physically shaken out of his absorption. It took him the whole flight back to Selene City to reorient himself into his own consciousness from the space beyond him or within him in which he'd lost himself. A very disturbing experience altogether. He wouldn't mind going home now. What more could the moon give him?

The trip back to Earth felt quite different than the flight out. Misha didn't mind being with the others. He actually enjoyed swapping impressions with them of the experiences they'd shared. When he didn't want talk, he stood by the window. Sometimes he looked at the stars, but more often he looked at Earth growing steadily larger in his sight. Its beauty pricked tears. This was beauty comprehensible in human terms: Misha could name its aspects. Earth was one. It was round. It was blue. It was mysteriously alluring under its changing cloud bands. Misha responded with love. He went to his hammock only to sleep.

When he got back to Calmar, he stopped by his apartment only long enough to make sure his tenant had cleared out as arranged and to pick up his rent. Then he caught a ziptrain to Devon Park.

He walked through the Park slowly, savouring its many wonders.

He felt a breeze on his cheek, the caress of living wind carrying assorted smells. Some were human smells, but he could actually scent water in it, a cool freshness from the river beside him. And colour. Everywhere colour glowing in the warm level light of evening. Much of it was people colour, artificial, but cheerful for all that. But some came from carefully fenced plots of grass or bushes or flowers, complex live colours, and some came from the sky itself. Had he ever properly looked at clouds and sky before?

And there was his tree. It was still alive! Misha pushed forcibly past the intervening people to stand in front of it. Its young summer leaves were intensely green in the mellow light. Its solid trunk held up its graceful branches for anyone who cared to look. Misha looked with deep love. Here was a beauty on his own scale. His tree wasn't big enough to diminish him — it just made him look up. It was other but not entirely, enduring but also changing, and alive, like Misha.

Misha inspected his tree. The disfiguring carving was not so blatant after a whole year's growth and a new spring. The weather had darkened the raw cuts to a colour close to that of the smoothed grey bark. The bark itself had grown in a little. In time, perhaps, he would be able to see the cuts only in memory. But if even the faint scars remaining proved too upsetting, why — Misha laughed aloud in joy and new amusement at himself — why, then he would stand and look at the other side! Misha reached out and gave the tree a featherlight kiss of a touch.

When he was nearly to the ziptrain station, his attention was caught by a display in an art supplies shop. A dummy in a colour-stained smock stood as if lost in thought before an easel. In one hand it held a palette blobbed with colours, in the other a brush. The easel supported a half-finished painting, startling for its vivid and strangely mixed colours. To the left of the easel a large colour wheel hung over a table, on which were scattered in careful disarray many tubes of oil paint, rags and interesting bottles. Fascinated, Misha looked at the painting, then at the paraphernalia that produced it. It might be fun to play with colours like that. What mixes could he produce? Could he make the vivid green the leaves were tonight? He looked for it in the painting on the easel. There. No, not quite. Maybe if.... After a few minutes, Misha entered the shop and spent all the money he didn't need for food on a box of oil paints, a bottle of turpentine, a pad of heavy paper and two brushes.

(RE) GENERATIONS

"Come camping with us this time — even for a short while," my son, Bryce, urges me, but I give him the usual excuses: I'm too old for a camping holiday; my legs won't hold up to the hikes the way they used to; I'd just interfere with their plans and make things uncomfortably crowded.

But this time he isn't taking "No" for an answer. "You're not old, Dad, and you're still in good shape. And the motor home has plenty of room for all of us."

"But — ," I start to protest.

"No buts. If you want to come home after a couple of days, I'll drive you back, but you're coming." He pauses, then, "It's six months since Mom died," he reminds me — as if I need reminding! "You can't stay at home mourning all the time. You need to get out of the house and get back some interest in life!"

I protest a little more, but finally give in. Maybe I'm just tired of arguing and thinking up excuses. Maybe what finally convinces me is the fact that the small, window-type air conditioner in my apartment quit three days ago in the middle of a hot spell. Whatever — I agree to spend a few days camping with my son and his family in the Spruce Woods

Park, on condition that, if I decide I want to return to the city, he'll put me on a bus, instead of driving the two hundred kilometres back.

The drive to the park is pleasant. My grandchildren, Annie and Jill, chatter excitedly about swimming and hiking, about looking for cacti and maybe seeing the elusive skink, an unusual type of lizard that Bryce has told them lives in the Spruce Woods. They're full of ideas, and only ask the dreaded "Are we there yet?" half a dozen times.

I remember another trip, the cross-country drive when my wife and I and four-year-old Bryce moved from Vancouver to Winnipeg, and he asked that question a thousand times. But the distance was much greater then, and the half-ton slower and lacking an air-conditioner.

I find myself reminiscing often, lately. Partly it's a generation thing, I think, but mostly it's since my wife, Annabelle, died suddenly last February. Now I do a lot of thinking about the old days — too much, some times. "You need to look forward, Dad," Bryce and my daughter-in-law, Sheryl, remind me often. "You're only sixty-two, Dad."

But some days, alone, sixty-two feels old. Not that I felt that way when Annabelle was alive. But when part of you — the best part of you — is suddenly wrenched away permanently, it makes you feel your years. I'm reminded of that as I help Bryce pull out the awning on the motor home, and then move the picnic table in underneath it.

"Come with us for a walk, Grandpa," my granddaughters urge, as soon as we've got things nicely arranged around the spacious campsite, but I put them off for now, sinking instead into one of the comfortable lawn chairs Bryce has arranged next to the campfire pit. The girls settle for riding their bicycles around the small camping loop, Annie's bike a regular two-wheeler, Jill's with training wheels still attached.

Annie — named for my wife — is six, her sister almost five. Both have their grandmother's auburn hair, but it is Jill whose small, round face so closely resembles Annabelle's. It is Jill whose smile can squeeze my heart in a vise, making me both happy and sad at the same time.

Their mother, in her usual efficient way, has brought a prepared stew for dinner. While she reheats it, I help Bryce clip down the red-checkered, plastic tablecloth, and tie a string between two maples for a clothesline. The wind is rising, soughing softly through the branches, a welcome relief to the heat of the last week.

Strange, but I'd almost forgotten how pleasant it is here. Annabelle and I visited a couple of times over the years. Not to camp — for Annabelle didn't like tents, and we couldn't afford anything like the motor home my son takes for granted — but just for a day's trip. We'd leave home early in the morning, packing a picnic basket with enough sandwiches and wieners for two meals, and set up at the beach or at one of the picnic tables in the day-use area, spreading towels and lawn chairs around as if to make the place ours. We'd stay until darkness or mosquitoes, whichever came first, drove us home.

"Come for a walk?" The girls beg again once dinner and the dishes are finished, but I shake my head. "I just want to take it easy tonight. Maybe tomorrow."

I see the look that passes between Bryce and Sheryl. 'Maybe we shouldn't have brought the old fellow,' they're probably thinking as they leave with the girls for a walk to the beach. I'm left to my own thoughts and my regrets — regrets that Annabelle and I didn't come here more often. I could have rented a motor home for a couple of days, if I wasn't so careful with my money. 'What was I saving for?' I wonder.

Shadows fall, and my family returns from their walk, the girls with sand in their hair and smiles on their faces. Bryce builds up a campfire, and we roast marshmallows until the breeze dies away, and mosquitoes begin their attack.

Later I lie awake, finding the bed strange, though not uncomfortable. Somewhere not too far away a single coyote howls, and farther off another answers. Later — much later — I hear the soft hoot of a horned owl, over and over, until finally I fall asleep.

Morning arrives much cooler, with a strengthening wind from the north. I pull on a heavy sweatshirt while Sheryl digs out jackets for the girls — Annie's a dull navy blue, Jill's a bright green that brings out the green in her eyes, and reminds me again of Annabelle. This time, after breakfast, I let them talk me into a walk to the playground. It's not the usual swings and seesaw, but a replica of a riverboat used on the nearby river a hundred years ago. We have to pass the beach to get there, but the breeze off the water is cold, the sky is cloudy, and nobody's swimming this morning.

The play boat is swarming with children. I find a bench and sit beside a young woman with a baby while Annie and Jill clamber over the various structures, wave at me from windows, and glide down slides, shrieking and laughing. I watch them half-heartedly, wondering how long before I can take them back to their parents, how soon before I can conveniently think of an excuse to take the bus home to my empty apartment.

It's strange, but while Annabelle was alive I didn't realize how much I depended on her for little things — like sewing a loose button on my shirt, or sending off the cheques to pay the monthly bills. These last six months, learning to do all the things she'd done, was like waking up some morning and finding you'd suddenly lost an arm over night. No wonder I spend so much time lying exhausted on the chesterfield or slumped in my easy chair beside Annabelle's matching one. Sometimes I even feel angry! How could she have left me to deal with all this alone?

"Much cooler this morning, isn't it?" The young woman beside me comments. But my answer is abrupt, and she doesn't try again to initiate a conversation I so obviously don't want.

When the girls tire of the boat structure, they draw me over to the campground store where I let them talk me into buying ice cream cones, even if it is only eleven o'clock. Jill tucks her hand into mine and smiles Annabelle's smile, chocolate covered, as we slowly meander back to the campsite.

"We've arranged to take the trip to the desert this afternoon," Bryce says when we reach the motorhome. "I hope it's okay with you, Dad. Sheryl and I will hike it, but we've bought tickets for the girls and you to ride on the wagon."

"I've been to the desert," I start to object. "And I don't need you to pay for a ticket." But he brushes my excuses off.

"It's too far for the girls to walk, and Sheryl and I really want to take the hike. This way you can help us, okay? We'll meet you out at the dunes."

After that, there's really no way I can refuse, and by shortly after 1:30 the girls and I are on our way to the sand hills, bumping over the rough trail in a wagon train type of conveyance pulled by a pair of plodding chestnut horses. The sun is shining but the wind is still cool, and we're all wearing jackets.

"Just as well it's cool," the driver says. "It can get pretty hot in the dunes with the sunlight reflecting off the sand."

The girls are excited but subdued by the presence of several other adults. They crowd close beside me, one on each side, watching as I point out the desert dunes in the distance, and the spruce trees partly buried by encroaching sand. The driver explains that this was once the delta of a great river, but the girls aren't interested in his geography lesson.

We reach the actual dunes ahead of Sheryl and Bryce, who are on a more circuitous route, and the girls scramble down from the wagon and hurry up the sandy trail to the top of the dune, urging me to "Come faster, Grandpa."

Stopping to catch our breaths — it's not just me doing the puffing — we gaze across the dunes, sweeping to north and west for a mile or so. In places, there is only sand; in other spots hardy, drought resistant grasses have prevailed, bending before the wind.

The girls run ahead again down the slope, then drop and roll in the sand, giggling together. I follow more slowly, watching as Annie reaches back to help her sister climb one of the slopes where grasses struggle against the choking sand. The wind ruffles her hair, and Jill's smiling "Thank you" to Annie tugs at my heart.

My shoes are full of sand and I stop to remove them, and soon I am carrying not only my own, but the girls' running shoes, too. I remember the first time I was here; it was Annabelle's shoes I carried then.

Bryce and Sheryl arrive, both out of breath. Sheryl is limping — "tripped on a root," she says — and her ankle is swollen. She sinks into the sand to wait while Bryce and I follow a short loop trail with the girls. Finally we head the reluctant pair back to the wagon, stopping to retie shoes.

"I can't do mine up," Sheryl says, limping a few steps, and it is obvious she is in pain.

"You'll never be able to walk back on that," I tell her. "You take my place on the wagon."

"Are you sure?"

"I'm not an old man!" I retort. "Even if I do look it!"

I give her my ticket, and Bryce helps her down the trail to the wagon. She is white-faced as he lifts her up beside Jill.

"You go, too, Daddy," Annie urges, pulling on his arm. "Then you can help Mommy get down again. I'll walk with Grandpa." And, after some discussion, we decide to work it that way. The wagon departs on the horse track, while Annie and I take the foot trail.

Winding around small hills and between stunted trees and bushes, the trail is not difficult, and we proceed slowly, stopping to examine a few wild sunflowers that, somehow, have managed to grow in the middle of a dune. At one spot several dead spruce trees, half-buried, lift skeleton arms to the sky. With a sense of déjà vu, I peer more closely at them, remembering another time.

"When your Grandma and I came before, that grove of trees was still alive," I tell Annie. "I have a photograph she took of that very spot. The sand hadn't got this far."

I wish now I'd brought her camera — but it's been on the shelf for six months — one of the many things I couldn't bear to look at.

We resume walking, trudging over roots that snake stealthily across the trail. Annie leads the way, and I follow, watching carefully where I place my feet to avoid roots and hollows. Suddenly a skinny dark shape, a few inches long, scuttles across in front of Annie and into a root cluster.

"What was that, Grandpa?" she shrieks excitedly.

We kneel down together and peer in between the roots just in time to see a six-inch brownish creature with black stripes disappear into the sand. Though I've not seen one before, I know at once what it is.

"It's a prairie skink," I say. "Do you remember what your dad said about them?"

"That the tail comes off?"

"Yes. If an enemy grabs it, it can escape by losing its tail."

"And then grow a new one, right?"

"Right."

I'm still crouched down at Annie's level, and I see her little forehead wrinkle with a puzzled frown. "What word did Daddy use for that?"

"Regeneration," I tell her.

She puts her hand on my shoulder and looks deep into my eyes. "Why couldn't Grandma's heart do that, Grandpa?"

Though we're two generations apart, our minds meet in mid-thought, and I know immediately what she means.

For a moment I'm speechless, and then I take a deep breath. "I'm afraid it doesn't work that way for people, sweetheart."

"It should."

"Yes, it should." Slowly I get to my feet, and we start the trek back.

It should, and maybe sometimes it does. Though the best part of my life has been wrenched away, maybe — soon — regeneration can begin.

AFTER THE SNOW

*D*elicate garlands of holly were still strung carefully from one side of the room to the other with tiny newborn treasures dangling in anticipation: a yellow rattle, lace bonnet, white baby socks, a soother and numerous other tokens of the seasonal variety for infants. Kimberly ignored them as she rested anxiously on her bed beside the large window. Outwardly unresponsive to the hospital environment, Kimberly raged inside like the swirling fury of last evening's snowstorm.

In the bed next to Kimberly's, another young woman softly hummed sweet lullabies. For the thousandth time, it seemed to Kimberly. Jenny smiled even when no one was there, and she didn't stop talking or singing to that baby she was carrying. Kimberly stared out the window at a chickadee scratching on the window ledge while light snow flurries put a finished look on last night's heavy snowfall. Amid the winter beauty, Kimberly regretted the life almost finished growing inside her. She didn't want it. She wasn't sure she wanted to be a mother, let alone a single mother. Kimberly wanted to scream at Jenny to stop singing those stupid lullabies, but she didn't because nothing was Jenny's fault. At least, none of Kimberly's problems were.

In the preceding few days, it had been a parade of visitors, of brothers, sisters, cousins, the usual and then some. Offerings of joy, of small gifts and goodies, adorned the long, narrow tables at the wall's edge. All glad tidings for Jenny.

Kimberly had no family. No family who wanted her anyway. Not even her ex-boyfriend Ian after five years together. Emptiness choked the expectant mother. What would this loneliness do to her baby?

Purely coincidental, both mothers-to-be were admitted to the hospital early because both were considered high risks. Two different kinds of risks. Jenny, a severe epileptic, had to be monitored during the last weeks before she would deliver. Kimberly had fainted too many times. The walk-in clinic obstetric doctor had insisted on hospitalization for Kimberly after discovering that this pregnant woman had hardly eaten for several weeks. The doctor's concern had been for the unborn child. She had no time for people like Kimberly. Irresponsible was the word used.

The two women shared the raw silence of needing to talk, but of not knowing how to speak to the other without offending or interfering. Strains of 'Silent Night' filtered in from the nurses' station down the hall. With Christmas just days past, why do they have to keep on playing those tired old Christmas Carols? wondered Kimberly.

"I think they do it to help us relax," Jenny offered cautiously. Kimberly winced. She must have spoken out loud.

"Oh."

"Music is good for the baby."

"That's why you're always humming."

"Yes," Jenny grinned, "I hope I'm not bothering you with it."

"Oh no." Kimberly lied.

"You'll get used to it," Jenny encouraged her roommate. "Being a mother and all." Kimberly felt her muscles tighten as Jenny's kind tone loosened the chains on her heavy heart, or was it contractions? Kimberly couldn't remember the last time anyone showed any concern for her. She didn't know how to react.

"I guess so." Kimberly didn't tell Jenny that she wasn't going to keep the baby.

"One of us will likely deliver the first baby of the new year. Shirley said there is a bassinet full of baby gifts and gift certificates for the first baby born after midnight of the first day of the new year. And you get your picture in the paper."

"Great." Good old Nurse Shirley! Kimberly hoped it wasn't her. She didn't want to be the lucky winner who takes all. She didn't want anyone to know she was in the hospital having a baby. It would make giving the baby up that much easier. "Your first?" Kimberly asked tentatively.

"Yes. Sixth generation on Johnny's side," Jenny beamed. "Normally, I take a lot of powerful medications but I refused to during my pregnancy. I couldn't let fear keep me from having a family. I have grand mal seizures: the bad ones. I wasn't supposed to have children at all but look at me now!" Jenny cuddles the tiny mound of baby within her. Kimberly couldn't understand anyone risking one life for another.

"Six generations is a lot." Kimberly barely knew her own father. Beyond that was a complete mystery to her. But there was her maternal grandmother who had tried to raise her — and there was her mother. The mother who had abandoned her early on.

There was also Ian, but he left her before she could tell him about the baby. Walk-in clinics and rooming houses were all Kimberly knew for the last seven months. She hadn't even tried to contact Ian. He had walked out on her.

"If it's a boy, we're naming him Silas after Johnny's great granddad." He turns one hundred on New Year's Day, and I'd say he's just about as young and strong as anyone our age. Great granddad is so excited about our baby. We'll take a generation picture for the baby book."

"What if it's a girl?" Kimberly inclined toward the neighbouring bed showing increased interest in the Jenny and Johnny family saga.

"Irene Elizabeth after my mother."

"Won't she be proud!"

"My mother died of cancer six years ago."

"Oh," Kimberly shuddered quietly, "I'm sorry."

"But you're right, Kimberly, she would feel very proud to know a granddaughter was named in her honour." Jenny smiled once more as she smoothed her delicate hands across the compact mound of baby. She began to hum again.

"You'll be a great mother, Jenny." Kimberly didn't know where her words came from. She never had intimate conversations with strangers. But she needed to tell Jenny what she thought. Their eyes met in silent contemplation about the wonder within that was soon to occur.

"You'll be a great mother, too." A quiet voice. A tightrope walker on a taut line. The words registered but Kimberly couldn't answer. "I heard the nurses talking when they brought you in here — " Jenny stopped abruptly, afraid to continue. She knew. Kimberly turned to look out the window again. "I don't even know this baby yet, Kimberly, but I know how much I love it already. My seizures have been bad the last couple of years and getting worse. Surgery might be my last hope, but that's also a great risk." Jenny pats her tummy. "Johnny and I prayed for this baby. Our miracle baby." Conversation lapsed as two soon-to-be mothers considered their situations. Tick tock tick tock went the clock at the nurses' desk. "I don't know how anyone couldn't love their own baby." Jenny didn't want to hurt Kimberly so she abandoned the conversation.

"I'm not keeping this baby." Kimberly's charged voice was barely audible but the message was clear. Ian had left her. She had no way of caring for a small life that depended on her knowing what to do. She didn't know what to do, and there was no one to help her learn. All she had known in her twenty-one years was struggle. Struggle and heartbreak. She wasn't mother material, but Jenny was. Kimberly was afraid to look across at Jenny so she continued to stare out the window at the snow falling. Snow was simple. It fell and it melted. There was nothing terribly complicated about snow. Simple and beautiful. And also dangerous. Recent raging snowstorms had everyone holed up in cozy homes and rooming houses. And hospitals. Yet after the snow, after the storms, sunshine often glittered over a breathtaking winter wonderland no one could have imagined. Cold hearts warmed.

"You haven't had it easy." Softly spoken. Understanding. Non-judgmental. Kimberly fought the surge of energy from deep inside her. Choked back emotion. Tears flowed anyway. Kimberly held her large stomach as tears rained down her face. Sobs demanded to be heard. An arm wrapped itself around her shaking shoulders. Jenny was beside her bed.

Kimberly awoke the next morning with the face of an old man staring into hers. A scream tried to find its way out of her throat but failed. She glanced at the empty bed beside her. Where was Jenny? "Good morning, miss," the old man offered.

"What are you doing here? Who are you?" Kimberly demanded gently. The old man smiled behind a mat of whiskers and beard. His eyes twinkled.

"I'm not Santa Claus." Kimberly smiled back. He certainly looked like he could be, except for the hospital robe and worn slippers. "To you, I will be Amos."

"Is that your name?"

"Do you like it?"

"It's a good name."

"Then my name is Amos." Kimberly didn't know what to think. Why would Amos be in the maternity ward in his pyjamas? "And you are Kimberly." He read the chart above her bed. Good eyesight for an old man, thought Kimberly.

"Yes."

"I see you've got a little package on the way." He nodded towards her immense belly mountain covered by warm blankets. Kimberly thought she should be offended by his intrusion, but the warmth of his personality spilled into her space, and she felt somehow comforted. "Your neighbour went for a walk down the hall." Kimberly was wondering if Jenny had gone into labour. "For a momma, you don't look too happy, but maybe it's just me."

"How did you get here?" Kimberly asked.

"Elevator from the third floor." Amos was serious. "But you gotta wait for old Bessie to get there, sometimes I'd rather take the stairs — except the alarm goes off. So I take the elevator." Amos was grinning. He had finished his explanation. "How did you get here?" Kimberly blushed.

"Well — "

"Well, now that's none of my business, is it?" Amos chuckled. "Nurses always telling me to mind my own business but — " he leaned in closer to Kimberly as though sharing a secret, "I hardly ever listen to them." Amos laughs at his own idea of a joke. "I can get around to twice as many people as they can in half the time when they leave me alone." He pulls a chair closer to the side of the bed. "Is it okay if I have a sit down for a minute?" Kimberly nods.

"Aren't you sick?" Kimberly questions the social stranger. "You're wearing your bathrobe."

"Nope, not sick. Healthy as two oxen and a bull in the barnyard. Just don't have any place to go. I'm old, and nobody wants me around if they have to care for me." He stresses the word care as if it were a disease. "I can't live alone, but I'm not sick. So I live in a room on the third floor. I've got money. I know how to cook. I just don't do it much. So finally they wouldn't let me go back home because I wasn't taking care of myself. I can't get into a seniors' residence because they think I'm too much of a risk, and I refuse to go into a nursing home. I've got a lot of spunk in me yet!" Amos dances a little jig with his long feet as if to demonstrate. "So I spend my time visiting here and there and driving the nurses crazy. How about you?"

"I'm having a baby." Amos jumps out of his chair like a fire were lit under him.

"You don't say!" Both laugh at Kimberly's joke on Amos. "Boyfriend leave you or something like that?" Kimberly drops her head and nods. "Damned fool."

"I didn't tell him."

"Well, now that changes things a bit. Don't you think he should know?"

"He left before I knew — for sure."

"And you want to punish him by not telling him about his baby."
Kimberly felt a jolt run through her as Amos said 'his baby'. She had
only thought of it as her baby when Ian was no longer there. Yes, she
was punishing Ian for leaving her alone with a baby on the way. But he
didn't know. It didn't matter. He had left her.

"You're only punishing yourself." Truth. Amos stares at Kimberly
for a long time with a lingering smile. "You're a smart girl."

He gets up to leave.

"Do you have to go already? I thought we were just getting
acquainted."

"Nurse Shirley will be after me with one of those mile long needles
she keeps stored under her desk for people like me." Amos places his
hand on Kimberly's. "Chin up, Kimberly. You've got a baby on the way."
Kimberly watches him go. She doesn't know what to think. She wants
him to stay.

Only hours earlier, Amos had been here, thought Kimberly, now she
had just gotten off the phone with Ian. Amos was right, Ian had a right
to know. Kimberly rolled her hands over the belly that would soon
disappear, over the belly that would soon mean a baby in her arms. Her
baby. Ian's baby. Their baby.

Jenny poked her head in the doorway. "Is it okay to come in?"
Jenny had insisted on giving Kimberly her privacy when she phoned
Ian. Kimberly couldn't believe his reaction on the other end of the line.
After she told him about the baby, there were sobs as Ian wept. Why
hadn't she told him? He wanted his baby. Their baby. Could he come to
the hospital to see her? Now as Jenny returned, Kimberly cried in her
joy. Joy of all joy. Ian really wanted to be with her. He wanted both of
them. Kimberly realized she was not alone. That she hadn't been alone.

"He's coming here. On Ski-Doo if he has to!" Jenny knew by the
look on Kimberly's face that things had worked out for the best so far.
"We're going to pick out names together."

What day was it?

Kimberly struggled to pull herself out of a dense fog. Aching. Pain.

Her head felt so heavy. Her limbs so numb. Kimberly knew when she opened her eyes that she was no longer in her room. She danced in and out of consciousness until a clear image came into view. Ian.

"Ian?" A hand reached out to hold hers.

"Yes, Kimberly, it's me." She felt different. Something was missing. The mountain was gone. She was afraid to ask but she had to know.

"Our baby?"

"A beautiful, tiny girl. They're looking after her." Ian's voice was comforting, but she heard the worry behind his words.

"Something's wrong." Kimberly noticed the IV hooked to her hand and some kind of monitor.

"Please, don't worry, Kimberly. She's fine. Both of you were too weak, so they had to take her out. You were bloated from malnutrition, and so was she. You both just need to rest for now. Our baby girl will be fine. She looks like you." Ian brushed the hair off Kimberly's forehead and kissed her. "Just rest."

Back in the room, Kimberly saw that Jenny's things were gone. Kimberly sat up in her bed and held her tiny bundle lovingly. The only Jenny thing left was a card Nurse Shirley had given Kimberly when she returned to her room. It was a card from Jenny. On the inside, Kimberly read the words scrawled in Jenny's large handwriting, 'I told you you'd be a good mother.' Nurse Shirley wouldn't talk about Jenny when Kimberly asked.

"Hi Honey." It was Ian. He had a pink teddy bear under his arm and pink carnations in his hand as he sailed through the door to greet his girls. "Hi, Baby Girl." He gently tweaked the tiny hand in the blanket. Kimberly was quiet. "You look more rested, baby." He leaned over to kiss her.

"What happened, Ian? Where is Jenny?" Kimberly demanded to know.

"She's gone home."

"There's more you're not telling me. I can tell."

"Kimberly — "

"Ian, please don't do this to me. I need to know the truth." Kimberly pleaded. Ian pulled his chair up close to her bed and took her hand. Kimberly fondly remembered Amos doing the same thing earlier. Ian's tender voice harboured a more serious tone as he rolled his head in his other hand, running his fingers nervously through his hair.

"Jenny's baby died. They didn't want you to know. You need to build up your strength, and they were afraid it would upset you to know."

"Jenny's baby died." Kimberly repeated the words as her heart stopped. She looked into the fuzzy blanket in the crook of her arm, into the face of the baby she wasn't sure she wanted at first. Jenny's baby died. Their only chance at a family. Their sixth generation. Kimberly felt wicked. Like she didn't deserve her baby. Poor Jenny!

"Jenny had an epileptic seizure that sent her into early labour. A grand mal, I think they said. It all happened so fast. The doctors and nurses did everything they could. I guess it wasn't meant to be." Kimberly began humming the tunes she had heard Jenny humming in the next bed. Wasn't meant to be! How could Ian even think such a thought! Jenny had wanted her baby. Kimberly studied the baby in the blanket on her arm. Studied the fingers all curled into little pink fists. Studied the eyes shut tight and the tiny little nose and the perky little mouth. A perfect little baby girl. Kimberly recognized the second chance she had been given. Realized how she had almost killed them both. But now she felt different. Ian hugged Kimberly gently as she wept for Jenny's baby.

"I want to call our baby, Jenny."

"Jenny's a perfect name."

"I have to tell Amos."

"Who's Amos?" Ian asked suspiciously. Kimberly laughed when she realized the cause of his concern.

"Oh don't worry, he's just a sweet old man who came to visit me. Amos is the reason I called to tell you about the baby. I just want to let him know." Just then Nurse Shirley appeared at the doorway.

"Time for rest now." She gently scooped baby Jenny out of Kimberly's arms to return her to the nursery.

"Shirley, I want to talk to Amos on the third floor. He came to visit me, and I want to thank him." Nurse Shirley looked confused. "A kind old man with a beard who doesn't have anywhere else to live. Do you know him?" Nurse Shirley still looked confused as she recognized the brief description.

"My dear, the only Amos on the third floor is in the later stages of Alzheimer's. He's not allowed off the floor because he wanders off. He doesn't have anywhere else to go anyway. Third floor has a stair alarm because of the Alzheimer's patients there." Kimberly was shocked. Nurse Shirley must be wrong. Amos had come to visit her.

"Sorry." Nurse Shirley left with baby Jenny. Ian tried to comfort Kimberly as much as he could but Kimberly persisted.

"How can that be? I want to see for myself."

"I don't think — "

"Ian, I need to see for myself; don't you see, Amos was the one who encouraged me to call you. If it weren't for him — " Kimberly didn't explain the rest. It would be better if Ian didn't know that she had planned to give the baby up after it was born. Plans had changed.

"Okay, I'll get a wheelchair and take you to the third floor." Somewhere in her heart Kimberly knew Nurse Shirley was right.

On the third floor, Ian inquired at the desk, then wheeled Kimberly down the hall to room 304. Piled in a heap of covers was a shell of a man wearing the same pyjamas that Amos had on when he came to visit. But Kimberly knew it wasn't her Amos. Her Amos was full of life. The man in the bed looked dead. Kimberly blew a kiss. "Happy New Year, Amos, and thank you." Amos wasn't there.

Silently, Ian wheeled Kimberly back to her room.

Ian had just left the hospital for the night when Kimberly's phone rang. It was Jenny. "Hey, Kimberly!" For the second time in a week, Kimberly felt joy. Pure joy. She thought of baby Jenny and couldn't wait any longer to tell her new friend.

"Jenny, I want to tell you something. You have a namesake." Kimberly listened to Jenny's happiness spill through the telephone lines. Kimberly talked about staying in the hospital until she was stronger, doctor's orders. Then she ventured, "Was it — ?"

"It was a boy. We named him Silas."

"I'm sorry."

"I know." A long silence followed. "Johnny says later we can think about adopting." Kimberly cringed. She had almost given baby Jenny up for adoption. The New Year's baby gifts she won seemed so insignificant now as Kimberly considered the difficult days Jenny had ahead of her. Kimberly would give every gift back if things could be different for her new friend. Amos had reached out to Kimberly, maybe Jenny needed Kimberly to reach out to her.

"Jenny," Kimberly hesitated, "I'll need — " She stopped. "I mean — " Kimberly had never expressed her needs to anyone before. Not even Ian. No one had cared much about her needs until now. Part of the problem that drove them apart. But Ian was back. They had decided to work things out. Kimberly thought of old Amos. Her Santa Claus in a way. Not the absent person she had left in room 304 melting away like the snow, but the Amos who had found her lonely and had led her back to Ian. As she listened for the young woman on the other end of the line, Kimberly realized that she needed Jenny to stay in her life. To be her friend. Jenny knew all about being a mother. It didn't occur to Kimberly that Jenny might need Kimberly, too. As Kimberly stumbled and stuttered over her words, she realized her friend knew what she was asking, but it was too soon. The memory and pain of loss would be close for a long time yet. Kimberly understood what Jenny couldn't say. Kimberly's baby had lived. Baby Jenny. A baby Kimberly hadn't wanted at first. In her grief, Jenny struggled with this fact.

"Soon, okay? Just not yet. I'll call you after the snow ends."

"Sure." Kimberly felt a new excitement growing in her. She felt a hunger for this new life opening to her. Jenny hadn't said no, hadn't turned her away. "Happy New Year, Jenny."

"Happy New Year, Kimberly."

JUSTIN FINDS A WAY

ustin, where are you? Your father'll be here in a minute."
"I'm out on the steps," Justin answers from the side of their
trailer on Maple Street. "I'm ready already. I been ready for
half an hour." 'Why doesn't mom call him 'my dad' like she used to when
he still lived with us?' He thinks. 'When I asked the other day why they
didn't get along, all she said was, "You'll understand when you're older.
It's easier to understand when you're older." Well, I'm going to be ten in
January. Maybe I can figure it out then.'

Justin waves to his best friend across the street; Scott, best friend
since kindergarten. Scott's father moved so far away, to Toronto,
they're lucky if they see each other once a year. Justin and Scott ride
their bikes together every day to school and back. They build jumps in
the parking lot and stooge around until their mothers come home from
work. Over at the mall, Justin gets Scott to help him scrounge wood
from the dumpsters. They pick out cans and bottles and get some
spending money, too. Yesterday Scott was planning what he'd do if he
had a million dollars. His blue eyes sparked and he rubbed both hands
in his blond hair.

"First," he said, " I'll buy tickets on a cruise ship so me and mom
and dad could go around the world."

Justin said, "Scottie, if you win some money or win a big trip how about taking me and my family with you? Wouldn't that be awesome?"

Justin checks his packsack for the third time. Everything he needs is there all right — extra runners and warm grey socks, blue jeans and the same kind of red plaid shirt he's wearing today. 'Wonder where dad is going to go to take pictures this time? Sure is neat when your dad is a famous, well, almost famous, wildlife photographer,' he thinks.

Justin knows more about birds than anyone in his class. At the beginning of the term this year, Mrs. Martin asked him, "Justin, how did you learn so much about birds?"

Justin answered, "My dad, he takes me to look for birds. He sells pictures of birds to magazines all over the world. That's his job. When I was little, before I went to school even, we used to go to the pond in the park. Dad gave me grain to throw to the mallards. They're the ducks with the shiny green heads. My dad says the males always have a white ring around their necks, and the females always make a lot more noise than the male ducks." Some of the children in the class laughed. Justin's face just got red.

"That's what my dad says. And he knows."

Mrs. Martin said, "Thanks you, Justin. Who else knows something special about a bird?"

Scott put his hand up. "Yes, Scott?"

"I like Canada geese, 'specially before winter when they're flying south. You hear them honking and you look up and see a big 'V' and you try to count them."

'Brrinng-ring' the closing bell clangs. As they walk down the hall, one boy tells Justin about a woodpecker that hammers on the side of his house every morning. It wakes him up before sunrise.

"I yell at it and it flies away. You can see black bars across its back."

"Does it have a red stripe on its face like a mustache?" Justin asked. "It might be a red-shafted flicker."

His friend laughs. " I'm so tired and so sleepy I wouldn't notice if it had a red beard."

A girl, who lives on the same street as Justin, joins in.

"We have hummingbirds every year. They like our trumpet vines on the back fence. All you can see of their wings is a blur."

Justin is thinking about some yellow birds that he saw this morning, not canaries — maybe finches. The sound of his dad's jeep interrupts his thoughts. Brown eyes shining with excitement he grabs his pack and gives his mom a quick hug. He thanks her for the two brown paper bags she hands him.

He can't take his eyes off his dad as they head towards the Okanagan highway.

"Where we going?"

"How are you, son?" They speak at the same time.

"I'm okay. Where are we going this time?"

"Up in the bush, Pennask Lake actually." Adding, " I remembered your sleeping bag. It's stowed in the canoe on the roof."

Justin nods. "Mom made us sandwiches and stuff. Enough for both of us." He continues, hoping his dad will ask about her, but they're in heavy traffic and his dad is concentrating on his driving.

Four hours later, they arrive at the lake and set up camp. Justin tries to stay awake after they eat supper. He's sitting close to his dad in front of the campfire, watching the flames. He can smell the damp forest behind them and hear the night wind in the pines.

Next thing he knows, it's morning. He can hear someone chopping kindling and, suddenly, the scream and splash of a loon out on the lake.

"Where is the loon, Dad?" he calls, as he stands outside the tent flaps.

"It's hard to see with all the mist. Here he comes. Guess he's looking for fish or frogs. Look at the checkerboard on his back. I should try to get an early morning shot." He puts his axe down and picks up one of his cameras.

The loon dives out of sight.

"Never mind. I'll try after breakfast. The light will be better anyway."

Justin eats scrambled eggs and toast in a hurry. His dad, with deft hands, lays out his cameras, films packs and lighting gear while Justin

115

starts to make cucumber and cream cheese sandwiches for them to take in the canoe.

"Stand still, Justin." His dad's warning voice is quiet but firm. "Stand still. There is a Canada Jay in the pine tree behind you. See if he'll come down. Hold a piece of sandwich out on the palm of your hand and see what happens."

Justin can hardly believe his eyes. A wild bird flutters over his shoulder. He can feel the claws as it clings to his fingers and snatches the bread from his hand and flies off with it. Justin, motionless, follows its flight with wide eyes. "What kind did you say it was, Dad?"

"It's a Canada Jay. No wonder loggers call them 'camp robbers'. You'd better wrap up all the food before he brings his friends and relatives and cleans us out."

But Justin is waiting. He has another piece of bread ready. Sure enough, the soft, fluffy, grey bird comes back. It floats down through the trees and pulls the bread from his out-stretched hand.

Justin's father aims the camera. He snaps three quick pictures. "Sure hope one of those turns out okay. You should see your face, son. You look like you invented sunshine."

On their way home next day, Justin asks his dad to send him a couple of copies of the jay pictures. That night Justin tells his mother about his weekend, except he keeps the best part to himself, the story about the wild bird that ate out of his hand. He doesn't even tell Scott what he plans to do.

Five days later, there is an envelope for him in the mailbox. Inside he finds a splendid close-up of an osprey carrying off a fish and another one of a pair of loons, but best of all there are two copies of him smiling in wonder at a small grey bird hovering above his outstretched hand.

Just then his mother calls and asks him to get a litre of milk from the store. Before he goes, he shakes some money out of his piggy bank. He wants to buy something from the store; it's part of his secret plan.

At the store, Justin buys two identical picture frames. He puts his two special photographs into them.

The next time his dad comes to pick him up, he gives him one of the framed pictures. Before he gets into the jeep, he gives his mother the other one. She says she'll put it on her bedside table. He remembers this as he's getting ready to go to sleep in his dad's apartment. Justin thinks about his pictures. One is on his dad's desk in the next room. The other one is beside his mother's pillow. It seems as if all three of them are together again.

THE BELL TOLLS
FOR ME, TOO

Mr. Cooke, my housemaster of five years in School House, entrusted me with the key to the bell tower for the purpose of manually and, hopefully, rhythmically tolling the bell to summon the population to church on Sunday mornings. I felt honoured that I had been chosen. I approached my newly acquired assignment with deep commitment and pride. For the longest while, I kept secret my destiny on Sunday mornings when I furtively climbed the stairs to the bell tower, quickly glanced both ways to be sure that no lost or bumbling 'new poo' had ascertained my intention, and hastily disappeared behind the door that lead to my domain of peace and solitude. I swore never to divulge to anyone, including even Bill McMahon, my roommate, that such a world existed, for privacy at Ridley was a scarce commodity, and for good reason.

The secret lasted two months. Not bad, considering all the eyes and ears housed in a boarding school. The darn thing was that it was not the eyes and ears that found me out; it was a nose. Erskine Carter smoked and, up until I undertook my sacred trust, Carter and I, and sometimes Cam McCool and Dougy, had shared a butt down the 'B' or the 'hogsback' on Sunday mornings. It was around the third Sunday of hauling on the rope that a deck of Rothmans slid from my breast pocket and landed at my feet. That morning, as you might guess, I had my first smoke of many in the bell tower. The thrill was immense; to think that I was casually dragging on a cigarette right in the heart of the school, feet away from masters and prefects, maybe even Ever Ready himself was passing by my door. Once I laughed out loud when I heard Victor Beany and John Howard appraising the continental cut of Mr. Carnegie's flannels. Cuffs were 'the in thing' in 1966, you understand; Derek Meany had said so, although Berrisford McConnel and Hume had disagreed.

The voices faded away and I ever so carefully destroyed the evidence, neatly folding the butt and ashes in the foil wrapper and gently tugging rhythmically on the ropes calling forth the populace to prayers. I pulled the chain to open a window high over head allowing the stale air to escape. After a few minutes of purifying the air and wondering at the complex arrangement of gears and dials that regulated the chimes every fifteen minutes from 7:30 in the morning to 10:00 at night, I shut the window and hurriedly left the bell tower with only one thing in mind: I needed toothpaste, now, to forever eradicate the last remnant of what was a serious offence punishable by caning.

Carter met me in the doorway of my room.

"You've been smoking".

I was done. He even went so far as to invite me to his room to listen to "The Whole World is Rapidly Changing," if I would only reveal my secret.

"Next Sunday," I told him, and in that instant I knew that was the beginning of the end. I had to tell him, for the inherent joy of the secret was in its revelation and now at least I had a partner to share in the crime. I would no longer be solely to blame, and my guilt would be lessened by a half as Carter had assumed ownership of the other half. Or so I thought.

Misfortune struck three Sundays later in the most serious way. We were pulling the chains to shut the last window when a pigeon entered and settled on one of the gears. We looked at each other and swore. We whispered "shoo" and "scat" and tossed our blazers into the air

120

attempting to frighten the dirty creature into flight and mercifully back the way it had come. It flitted to another gear, defecated two times with a flick of the tail, and settled comfortably, all the time cooing softly. We had a quick discussion and decided that our best course of action was to leave the window open so the bird could exit voluntarily. We had no doubt that our uninvited guest would be soon longing for the great outdoors and the companionship of the flock that enjoyed the open spaces between School House and the Chapel. We scraped up the white stuff from the floor and hurried to Chapel for some serious prayer. I couldn't speak for Carter, but I knew that I was going to be meditating on more than big Lillian in Jamaica or cricket against T.C.S. For the rest of the day, I was swept along by the human tide that was directed unforgivingly by prefects and schedules and housemasters and bells. No time for anything of my own. No opportunity to submerge temporarily to deeper and darker places. I glanced but once at my door, only to be carried onward toward the end of the day and lights out. I lay in bed imagining the worst: the bell tower had become the domain of the pigeons, and what of the mess! But maybe good fortune was on my side. Nothing had happened yet. I'd done a lot of praying, too. And Carter had said it was okay. So I slept. He owned a half, a full half....

It was 2 o'clock in the morning when I sat bolt upright in bed. There was a great irregular bonging ringing in my ears. Our room was only yards from the bell tower and in the still of the night the noise was overwhelming, a terrific cranking and hammering from above. McMahon merely grunted. When the noise ceased, I babbled out my story hoping for some comfort in return for my confession. But he said nothing and we lay in the dark thinking on what had happened and what might yet happen. Finally McMahon said, "You're screwed," and just as abruptly went back to sleep.

The chimes rang irregularly and out of tune all through Monday and quite into Tuesday. Each time I cringed in terror; I certainly was being punished for my sins, and yet no one approached me although every time I went somewhere I took the long dark tunnels from place to place, always on the lookout for Cooke. Monday evening, I mustered all the courage in my tormented being and returned to the scene of the accident. My once private domain was now a big toilet of bird dirt and feathers. Those pounding chimes had shaken out the loose feathers and set the bowel to trembling. I retreated forever, beaten by the pigeons of School House.

Finally at lunch on Tuesday, I asked haltingly, "Did anybody hear the bells?"

I caught the unmistakable look in their eyes that they knew. Yes, indeed, I was screwed. Why not 'fess up forthwith? Why this unseemly denial? I was searching for a way out when Mr. Carnegie volunteered, "Oh, you mean the School House ghost? Back to his old tricks again."

"Must be," I mumbled, "the School House ghost is on the prowl again." This was a most timely turn of events. Saved by the bell!

"Not so funny," he countered the looks of incredulity. "A teacher died in the bell tower in 1918 from influenza. There was an epidemic."

TWO FOND HEARTS

hen I was a girl in Wales and our choir-master, Mr. Emlyn Reese, told us about *Lily*, I thought my heart would drown within me.

After Chapel that Sunday morning, Mr. Emlyn Reese stood up from the piano seat to announce that all the girls nine years old and up to thirteen should stay back. Mam glared over at May and me, as if staying back was our idea.

But she could see all the other girls were getting to stay. It was Chapel after all and Mr. Dai Roberts, our preacher, must have known about whatever was happening — even if he had stepped down from his tall desk, and was now waiting on the chapel steps to shake hands with folk leaving. So nothing was left for Mam to do, but let me and May stay.

As she and Da passed us on their way towards the big chapel door, Mam hissed in my ear, "Look you, mind you two come straight home after. There's potatoes to do." And I nodding, nodding, May giving a long-nosed toss of her head — after our mam turned away.

Da winked at me and May and off he went too, offering his arm in a swoop to our mam as if he were King Edward and she, a princess and not just our mother. The two of them were that fond, sometimes when I watched them I felt I was standing outside Aldani's Sweet Shop, looking at chocolate whorls through the glass without a farthing in my pocket. And Mam took Da's arm and smiled with her eyes, although her lips were rulered straight across. Mam knew her proper Chapel face, if anyone did.

May and I edged about on the hard seat, and I wondered what was coming. Ada Bishop from my class at school was there, and both the Harry girls, looking like raisins, puckered and dried up in ugly brown dresses. Their mam made their dresses out of hers and Mrs. Harry could hardly sew a straight seam.

Even at ten, I knew good dressmaking to see it. I had already worked a sampler hanging on the rose-papered wall in our parlour over the velvet settee:

Let not your hands go idle.

What I had ached to stitch in red floss was:

The Devil finds work for idle hands.

But when I asked Mam, she said "No," and narrowed her eyes as if I had dared cheek her in front of the neighbours. "We don't use such words in this house, leave alone hang them on the wall for the minister to see!"

Anyway, in Chapel that morning, May's friends Cassie and Meghen were there and Catrin and some others older than me — about twelve or thirteen of us girls. Some of us looked scared like we were already in trouble, and some just sat picking at their fingernail skin. Some — bold as brass they were, like our May — looked straight on at Mr. Emlyn Reese standing in front of us and then he was the one to blush, wasn't he.

I remember our choir-master as a plump young man who wore a high black vest with pearl buttons and a proper black tie about his neck. Lovely he always looked, his hands all tender-looking and clean — even under his fingernails, when he waved them about, leading the choir. His skin was soft and white, the kind that shows the blood rising underneath. I saw the red myself when we met him in the draper's where he was a shop assistant and he came over all flustered, to serve Mam. A pink and quivery nose when he talked but oh, such a voice he had singing!

He sang tenor did Mr. Emlyn Reese, with the notes so high and pure it made your teeth ache with the sweetness. He would throw his head back and let the song ripple through his throat in great up and down swells until the tears came to your eyes. He was mostly a short man, but whenever he sang he stood taller than anyone and his voice climbed to God sitting up there in the beams above our heads.

Oh, fond I was of Mr. Emlyn Reese when I was ten. That is often the way with little girls when young men are kind to them and demand no bravery from them. Perhaps I knew in him a shyness greater than my own. And oh, how I shivered to hear the lark notes pouring from his throat if I should be in Chapel when he was showing the choir the tune: *la, so, fa, doh, doh* — that is what we did in those days, how we learned tonic sol-fa. That is really why I went to Scripture Class on Wednesdays, why I stayed back a little longer — to hear Mr. Emlyn Reese singing, isn't it.

My father, John Jones Treharris, himself was famous for singing and every Sunday he said after Chapel, "Well now, Mrs. Jones," — that was our mam — "that Emlyn Reese lad may be young but he can pull the music from us right enough." Da was still singing in the Male-Voice over the mountain in Treharris. Won competitions did our Da, before the black spit took him over.

Now on that Sunday, our May said, cheeky as you please — she was wearing her new grey coat with the black velvet collar; it would be quite worn out by the time I got it — thought herself something, did May, always had a word ready hot like a potato in her mouth, anyway she said, "Why have you kept us back, Mr. Reese? My mam said I was to hurry home."

And Mr. Emlyn Reese doing his best to look important, but flooding red and stammering a bit, his baby little cheeks all bouncy, "There is something I want to tell all you young ladies." Squirming on the benches, smothered giggles.

"Next month I am putting on an operetta, one I have written myself, both words and music," he said, jittering about on his little feet. "I call my operetta *Lily*."

Everyone stilled to stare blankly at him. Everyone except my sister. May turned pitying eyes upon the rest of us. "That is something like an opera, people sing the story, not talking like in a proper play," she said.

"Well, to be sure, in a way," said Mr. Emlyn Reese, redder than ever, stopping still, stopping his dance. That May. Always the clever one.

"I thought if I told you about it, the story, how it works, you might..." he went on uncertainly, "When the curtain goes up, there is a poor little orphan girl Lily on stage, all alone, singing. She lives by herself in a cruel, cold city where she must sleep in shop doorways. She sings on the streets for pennies, to keep body and soul together."

As Mr. Emlyn Reese went on, his voice gathering strength, I could picture poor Lily — such a beautiful name Lily; I would die to be a Lily instead of a Rosie — singing her throat out, bending to pick up pennies from the pavement, however many the whiskery men threw at her feet. Such a rough lot they were coming out of the rich men's club; I could picture them winding their big gold pocket-watches on pure gold chains, no shame in them to see a ragged orphan child out in the dead of winter with only a thin little shawl about her poor, brave shoulders.

Oh, it was all I could do to keep from weeping, right in front of Mr. Emlyn Reese. There's glad I was I could sop up my tears in my handkerchief, I couldn't have done with teasing. Bad enough, the big lads at school said terrible things to me — like that Richie Phillips who sat behind me and pulled my hair when Miss Evans was not looking. Him whispering dirty things — Rosie give us a kiss — and who could I tell?

Our mam would snap *ach a brwnt* and look at me as if I were the dirty one, not Richie. Our May would stare down her nose at Richie and that would stop him.

I had turned ten. I shouldn't need to ask someone else for my spine, they said.

Anyway, in the operetta it all comes right in the end. Mr. Emlyn Reese said, his voice all quivery, he was that fond of Lily, "In Act Two, when Lily lies near to death on the cold road and it is snowing — we shall have to think of a way to have the snow come down — a rich stranger comes along and finds Lily lying on the road clutching an old silver locket. This is a kind, rich man and when he opens the locket, he finds a picture of his dear wife who was kidnapped with their baby daughter years ago. He is Lily's dear father, and when he discovers his dying little girl, he sends someone for the doctor."

It seems the doctor comes along and gives Lily medicine, then everyone is singing and Lily sits up and sings too, in a new coat with a fur collar her father happened to have in his suitcase.

Beautiful it was, the story. Even May had tears in her eyes, although her mouth trembled at the corners, and she was choking a bit so she could have been laughing in that nasty, boiled-sweet way she had.

"Now then," said our choir-master, "I have some folk in mind for the father, for the choir. But I don't have my Lily, and she is most important. I shall hold auditions for the part of Lily tomorrow night before Young People's. I hope for a big turnout of you, young ladies. Be ready to sing a little song for me. Lily must have a very good voice for so many solo selections! Tell your friends."

"Mr. Reese," said Ada Bishop with a prettily worried face. "My mam would never let me be in a play. Plays are the Devil's work, my mam says. They don't let me go to the pictures either. Not that I would want to. That is the Devil's work, too." Ada chewed over Devil, close to saying a bad word, and so brave to say it right in Chapel!

A few other heads nodded.

"Oh dear to goodness Ada, you must tell your mam this is not a play. This is an operetta. With music! It has a very strong moral lesson. There's singing!" For Mr. Emlyn Reese, singing was triumph enough over sin.

Ada Bishop sat back, meekly smug. Ada had a true voice and was chosen at school to sound the tuning fork to pick up the note for singing. Ada had long golden hair tied back with a red butterfly bow for school, a blue one for Chapel. The blue fluttered on top of her head at that very moment, making her taller, even more beautiful. Suddenly, my

127

insides went dull, and my shoulders slid down the back of the bench. Why try? Certain it was Mr. Emlyn Reese would end up picking Ada Bishop for his Lily.

"Are you going to, May? Try out?" That was May's friend Cassie skipping about excitedly at the bottom of the chapel steps.

"I expect so; it might be interesting. I'm coming out to Young People's anyway." May was old enough for Young People's.

"I am going to try, too," said Cassie, her black eyes shining. "Such a lovely story. That poor Lily."

And off the two of them went up the High Street arm in arm, not even waiting for me. No-one even bothered to ask if I was interested and all at once I made up my mind to try out, too, even though just thinking about singing alone made my stomach pinch. I knew Ada Bishop would end up playing Lily, but I could be in Mr. Emlyn Reese's company, have him look just at me, wave his clean hands at me.

When Mam heard why we had stayed after Chapel, I wasn't sure if May or I could even get to see the performance, leave alone try out.

"An operetta! In Chapel?" Our mam's voice was raspberry jam, sweet and red jelly on top with hard seeds like pebbles beneath. Whatever she said seemed to stick in your teeth like raspberry pits. Da got Mam's soft sweetness, May and I got the stones.

"Whatever is that Emlyn Reese thinking of?"

"It's not going to be in Chapel, Mam. It will be held in the Miners Institute and there's a good moral to the story. There's singing!" declared May, sounding for a moment just like the choir-master.

"If there's to be singing, Gladys, then I see no harm." That was Da, our treacle man, our lovely man. "Let them try out. Good it is for young people to put themselves into a singing competition; it makes them sing their hearts out. If they don't come first, there is still pleasure in hearing the fine voices, isn't it."

A true Welshman, that was our Da, and he would have sung until the day he died if his lungs had let him.

"As you say then, John." Our mam would never go openly against Da. "Not that either one will be chosen in any case. May is clever enough, but she has no voice. And Rosie would never remember what to do; she would fall about in a panic to be on a stage. You'd never hear a peep out of her, such a rabbit she is." Mam was speaking Welsh to Da. She called it *cwningen*, "rabbit" and rolled her eyes.

"Oh, now," said Da.

My cheeks flared heat. I looked at May sideways from under my eyelids. May's face was pale, and her eyes snapped sparks, but she kept her mouth shut — for fear of losing advantage, I suppose.

I wanted only to run. Upstairs, out the door, up the road, into the fields. Instead I set about to peel the potatoes waiting in the basin. As I stabbed the knife into the furry brown skins, the words ran round and round in my head: you'd never hear a peep out of her — such a rabbit, rabbit, rabbit.

"*Cwningen*". That was what I was. At school, I pulled myself quiet into my seat and worked without raising my head, for fear of meeting a boy's cheeky eye or a frown from Miss Evans. At school, I hated the breaks and prayed for rain, when we could stay inside the building and draw on any bits of paper we could lay hand to.

Then I could make flowers and animals come alive, first in my head and then on the paper. I grew such roses and daffodils, bluebells and heather, tiny, tiny around the paper edge, that way you had room left in the middle for another rainy day. I loved to sketch birds, cats, rabbits, hoarding in my head what I saw in the fields and the woods — the way feathers rippled like little seas on a bluebird's back, the way hairs rayed out in glistening suns within rabbit fur. On Friday afternoons, we sometimes were let to paint watercolours and then I crept to another place within myself. Oh the joy to mix colours, to have clean pages waiting, to use my brush with precisely flowing strokes. I was bold then, brave Rosie alone.

One of the teachers, Miss Mavis Jones, brought a notebook to school and asked me to paint for her. On the cover! I'll never forget those flowers, bluebells they were; I loved the shy blue, like the sea with secrets deep inside.

On Monday after tea, May and I went to the tryout. I told myself I was old enough, strong enough. I told myself it would be as Da said, "No matter who gets chosen, it will be lovely to hear the voices."

Myself sneered back, "*Cwningen*", and my feet dragged on the road, so that May turned to snip, "Hurry, can't you?".

Quite a few of the Chapel girls were there already; some older girls I recognized from school and Ada Bishop, wearing her blue butterfly, and her Chapel skirt although it was only Monday. She slid onto the bench next to me, and I swear I could smell scent on her although I knew Ada's mam would never have let her wear scent.

"Whatever are you going to sing, Ada?" That was Cassie, leaning around me.

"I shall sing 'Praise I Will Ever Give to Thee,'" said Ada, virtuously. "We are in Chapel, after all."

"Oh, right you are," said Cassie, her round face straight. "Then I had better change mine. I was going to sing one about girls' knickers. Jack taught me." Jack was one of Cassie's older brothers, all of them working the coal face. And she and my sister went into a shaking of giggling, there's shame, and Ada stared at them and moved away to another row.

Meanwhile, my heart sank. Why hadn't I thought of that? Mr. Emlyn Reese would only want to hear chapel music and I had planned to sing 'Two Fond Hearts' — '*Tra bo Dau*'. Our Da was always singing it about the house to our mam, pretending sheep's eyes at her until she slapped at him but you knew she was that fond, she didn't mind, and her fingers always stopped a bit on his arm. So I could sing Da's song either in Welsh or English, whichever Mr. Emlyn Reese wanted. So I had thought.

Now a cloud settled over me, and I was so nervy already I had no spit in my mouth but must keep clearing my throat until it felt raw in my neck. Perhaps I should just go home. But then I remembered Mam and her *cwningen* and her rolling eyes. I trembled like a rabbit scenting dogs, but I stayed on the Chapel bench.

And then Mr. Emlyn Reese came bustling in. Each of us were to go to the front and stand below the preacher's high desk to sing while Mr. Emlyn Reese stood at the back of the Chapel near the door.

"I want to judge how well the voices carry," he said. "And who will go first?"

Ada's hand shot up and she paraded to the front and turned to face us, blue butterfly hovering. Her face shone in demure self-satisfaction. Then she opened her mouth, and I could forgive her anything for the pale true notes from her lips. She sang one verse and chorus. Then she pulled out both sides of her skirt into black wings and curtsied.

"Very nice, thank you, Ada. Who is next?"

And so it went. May sang *Cyfr'r Geifr* 'Counting the Goats', but Mam was right, May's voice screeched a little on the high notes, even with her being so clever. Then Cassie sang something, I can't remember what, except it had nothing to do with girls' knickers. And then others sang, and some were worse and some were better, but none better than Ada. Nobody else curtsied.

And then it was my turn, and my bones seemed to have turned to water under my skin.

"Now Rosie," said Mr. Emlyn Reese. "Are you ready, *bach*?"

'*Bach*', 'little one'! That was what Da called me. And suddenly it was just the choir-master and me in the Chapel, and that lovely man had called me his little one, had given me my spine.

"I shall sing '*Tra bo Dau*' for you, Mr. Reese," I spoke clearly from the front of the Chapel, standing in the shadow of Mr. Dai Roberts' big preaching desk. And I opened my mouth so that my heart could come singing up my throat to fly over to Mr. Emlyn Reese standing back in the dusk of the big room.

'Beauty will pass like a shadow
Wealth is elusive and vain
True love is strong and lasts as long
As two fond hearts remain...'

I could hear myself singing, but I could also see myself standing, easily, lightly. I remember thinking, "This is how God sees us from above." I could see the girls in front of me but they didn't matter. I wanted to sing into every corner of the room and bathe the dim figure at the back with my true love.

When the last note was sung, I came slowly from somewhere else — some meadow in a far-off woods — and was back in my own body again.

Then my kneecaps started to shake under my skirt, and I had to hurry walk and plop myself back down on the bench and hide my trembling hands under crossed arms. May stared at me as if she had never seen me before and Cassie squeezed my arm in a kind pinch.

Mr. Emlyn Reese cleared his throat several times, then moved to the front of the Chapel.

"Well now, well now, this is very difficult, young ladies. You have all done splendidly and I thank you for turning out. I trust you will all attend the performance to encourage your friends. Now you are anxious no doubt to know who will play Lily. I have decided my Lily will be — " Mr. Emlyn Reese stopped, and I thought my choked breath would burst through my chest — "Rosie Jones."

Words followed about rehearsals and meetings, but I could think only in blurs. I remember Ada Bishop's thin lips and how her butterfly seemed to have shrunk to the size of a shilling. I was Lily! I would see Mr. Emlyn Reese every night. He would call me *bach*. And Mam would know I had been brave. I was not a rabbit!

I ran up the High Street ahead of May. I couldn't wait a minute longer to tell my news.

"Mam! Da! I am Lily," I cried even as I burst through our front door and ran down the dark passageway to where my mother and father sat at the kitchen table next to the lamp. "I got chosen. Mr. Emlyn Reese picked me!" I hopped up and down.

"Well, now," said Da, putting down the *Caerphilly Journal* and smiling.

Mam looked up from the school stocking she was mending. She

was silent for a moment while she looked about for the scissors and finally cut the yarn viciously with her teeth.

"Hmph," she snapped, stopping to squint another strand of black yarn into her big needle. "Then the others must have been bad."

I stopped still, frozen like a rabbit caught out in the middle of a field. My head emptied itself of words. At the same time, I saw my Da turn and stare at our mam as if he had just met her for the first time.

She caught his stone gaze and said defiantly, "There's wicked it is, a sin unto God, a child with too much pride."

My Da said nothing for a long minute, then he spoke to her and she daren't turn away from his eyes, even though so much fire was in them. She must be burning up, yet his voice seemed cold, "There is pride and there is pride, and our little Rosie has done well and shown her spirit. We should be praising God for that spirit for she will need it, as will we all." And he kept on looking at her, and after a bit her eyes dropped away first, which never happened in our house.

Then Da sighed and the fire in him died out. He turned back to me. "What did you sing, *bach*?"

"'*Tra bo Dau*', Da. I tried to sing it the way you do to Mam," I said shyly.

"Well done, my little one. Let us sing it together right now."

So we sang, Da and I in that dim room with Mam looking down at her hands folded over the black stocking in her lap. And as we sang — our two voices flying up like two birds matching wing beats — two tears rolled down Mam's cheeks, and it was the only time I saw my mother cry when there was no good reason.

HIGH WIRE

*R*ight to the bottom they say he jumped. That was our Eddy, his one last stunt.

We all lived here in Tiggleston then, a bunch of us retired circus people. Besides Eddy, there was Freaky Fern, the old sideshow woman who'd weighed six hundred pounds before joining the weight loss group in the community hall. There was Jethro Coombs from the elephants, and trick rider Prissy Gallant, and then there was me.

* * *

Like their parents before them, Eddy and his twin sisters, Tina and Darla, were trapeze artists. When I was just ten days old, my mother Carmel, an assistant to Hook the lion-tamer, ran off with a man from Niagara Falls. In the note she left, she'd told Hook that I was all his, but Hook swore it wasn't so, so Eddy's mother took over, and I ended up on the high wire.

Throughout the years, the troupe expanded from summer tent affairs to big new arenas nationwide. A mishmash of carnival and circus. And we were expected to perform more daringly, give the audience more of a thrill. Not just trapeze. Motorcycles were brought in, and Eddy and I flew them across thin cables up near the rafters. A heart attack each time for me, though Eddy loved the excitement, the tease of death.

It wasn't a bad life, really. Sometimes after performances, Eddy and I and his sisters would borrow a circus bus, and end up in some honky-tonk bar. Once a leather-faced, drunked-up woman in a cowboy hat grabbed Eddy for a dance. Taken aback by his arm muscles, she hooted that he must really work out. Feeling no pain himself, Eddy hooted back and said, 'No, Ma'am, he'd never set foot in a gym, but did she want to see a daredevil at work? Did she want to see a really good show?' He told her he was the goddamn best in his profession, and to come and see for herself. And so she did. And followed him around for the next three months. Off they'd roar in her red pickup late at night, and Eddy so drained the day after, but you could tell he was happy. There was that contentment in his eyes. Until one night, she stopped showing up and Eddy began brooding.

The years passed, and so did our energy, our stamina. Sometimes Eddy would break out in tears. He didn't have it anymore. Timing gone all to hell. Almost missed catching Darla on the swing. Or, he'd dropped down into the net during practice. What was he going to do? On and on he'd go, feeling sorry for himself, and the boss down his neck. I, too, was pumping myself full of vitamins, trying to keep up. So in my head, I began devising a plan. A lot of us were no spring chickens. And me with a troublesome rhomboid muscle, it was only a matter of time before I, too, would be done with the high stuff. So why keep on?

I spoke to my friends Fern and Prissy first. Let's get off this merry-go-round, I suggested. Settle in some small place where we'd have a taste of real life. For none of us could remember much other than the circus life. Maybe some winters penned up in a couple of rooms somewhere, waiting out the weather, back in the days when our schedules weren't so gruelling. Oh, to have a bedroom, a proper kitchen where I could cook myself some eggs, and a nice chair to sit in and watch TV, why it would be like having a million bucks in the bank! Think about it, I said, and they convinced Jethro to join us. Even Eddy, who'd been skeptical of the idea, who didn't want to leave without his sisters — and they were staying put — eventually gave in. By then he'd broken off with Gerda from costumes, anyway.

So a few months later here we were in the village of Tiggleston, population 512. A sprawling white frame house rented from the township dogcatcher, bargain furniture, and our pensions starting to drift in. Life! Prissy missed her ponies for a while, but only until she got into the local solo club, and Fern, like I said, joined the weight loss program. Jethro got bored being in one place, and when the circus wouldn't take him back, he took off for Africa. Lots of elephants there, he said. Me, I just relaxed. Bought an old jalopy, put some beer in the fridge, and just puttered.

It was Eddy that the move was hardest on.

Gradually, after we left the troupe, he shut down. Stopped talking, eating properly, even shaving. "He's just a tad depressed," Fern said. "He'll get over it; you watch and see." So I left him to his thoughts, and went out in my car every day. It was the start of summer, already hazy and hot. I stumbled around the stores in the nearest town, did what normal people seemed to do. At Zeller's I bought shirts on sale, a pair of Brooks running shoes, at Canadian Tire a bag of water softener salt. I talked to cronies in the doughnut shop, guys like myself who didn't know what to do with their time. I said I was a retired garage mechanic. Or a welder. Sometimes a used car salesman. A whole lot easier than explaining the truth. Do you good to get out, too, I'd say to Eddy, but all I'd get was a stare and a glare.

And so it went, until, suddenly, just before Christmas, he started talking again. He'd gotten a card from Tina and Darla, and some photographs of them hamming it up.

"See, what I said's true," Fern stated a few days later. "Eddy's coming around." She was setting out three plates at the table, and her arm flab swung like clock pendulums. Lately, she'd been filling up empty Javex bottles with water, lifting them to improve her muscle tone. I'd been scanning the papers for a set of used weights for her.

Prissy was hardly ever home by then, having discovered the local tavern and its patrons. She'd also discovered she could sing, and so three nights a week, she belted out tunes at the karaoke, dressed up in her sparkly trick-riding outfits.

About this time, too, Eddy started pigging out. He'd trudge down to the general store and bring home little packages of pepperoni sticks, hunks of farmer's cheese. He scarfed down big bags of chips, jumbo size bottles of Coke.

"You keep this up, yer gonna look like me soon," Fern scolded. "Which some days is worse than death." Poor Fern, for all her hard work at dieting, still had trouble breathing, doing steps, walking any distance.

* * *

Weeks went by, and a blizzard blew through the countryside. There was snow up past the fence lines, and schools were closed, even churches. We ran out of Carnation milk for our coffee, and the village store ran out, too. After four days, the weather let up, and the sun came out and things got pretty well back to normal. At least, it seemed that way to me. Spring arrived finally, and then one day when Fern was out getting weighed, and Prissy was at her card club, I asked Eddy if he wanted to go with me to the circus. I'd heard on the radio that our old gang was performing nearby. By this time, Eddy's once slight frame had ballooned. He now had a big belly, fat rounded shoulders, and a doughy face. But for a second, there was a gleam in his eyes, and his forehead creased, and I could tell he was thinking. I hoped his answer would be yes, because it would be like old times again, only better. We'd be spectators. And it was a chance to catch up on the circuit news.

So I was real disappointed when his eyes filled up with tears, and he shook his head. "Naw, you go on without me," he said. And he rubbed at his bald spot and the strands of grey fuzz surrounding it. For a minute, he sat there, staring down at his ratty slippers, but then he hoisted himself out of his chair and went into his bedroom off the kitchen.

I could hear him opening drawers, shuffling papers, and soon he brought out an envelope. "See that Tina and Darla get this. I put a note in." It was sealed, but I felt the bulk of bills in it. Eddy had never trusted banks.

"You sure they're still working?" Eddy had not mentioned them since Christmas.

"They'll be there." And he disappeared back into his room, and that was that.

* * *

So I bought myself a ticket and went. I gave the envelope to Tina afterward, who gave me a tight hug and asked a hundred questions about us all.

"Be sure and stop by before you hit the road." I turned to go, then thought differently. "Better still, why not now? Surprise the old boy."

And so Tina fetched Darla, and I drove them in my T-bird back to the house, and we roused Eddy from his La-Z-Boy where he'd fallen asleep. He muttered something in Ukranian, but after his surprise at seeing his sisters he grinned. By then Fern and Prissy were home, and Prissy made some ham sandwiches and I passed around the Molson Golden.

We sat out in the kitchen, telling old carnival jokes, sharing memories. Darla told of Phoenix the fortune teller warning a middle-aged woman to watch out or she'd be getting pregnant, and the woman screaming at Phoenix, yelling that didn't she know all her parts were gone. Fern hee-hawed till she nearly choked.

On and on well past midnight, with Eddy shifting his eyes from sister to sister. Nothing was said about the envelope I had given Tina. Had it been opened? I did not know.

"Come on, you girls, you can bunk here for tonight." Over the years, I'd been known to creep in with one or the other, no big deal. But just then I was feeling too tired and woozy to drive them back, let alone try any horseplay. Fern and Eddy were yawning, too, and Prissy was clattering around the kitchen, trying to make coffee.

Darla gave me a sly smirk, poked me in the belly and said maybe that wouldn't be a bad idea, but Tina huffed and puffed and said, 'Nope, we'd better get back to the trailers." Giving Darla a meaningful stare. So I got my jacket.

Darla gave Eddy a smooch on the top of his head, and as she brushed past me, I had an unexpected yearning for our old life. Not just for Darla herself, but everything. Of roaring a bike across a cable. Of the terror and exhilaration of sweeping through the air, of gauging the moves, of connecting at precisely the right second. The exactness of it all, the skill required. The suspense. The heady knowledge that hundreds of eyes were fixated upon you, hundreds of hearts were clutched. And in that moment, I knew what Eddy had been missing. Maybe it had all been a mistake, this brainy idea of mine, to give it all up.

I was still thinking about this as I drove the women back. Listening to them talk about their next gig, and about how they still couldn't picture Eddy now living smack-dab in the country. "Remember how he used to be scared of spiders?" Darla laughed, her beery breath exploding on my neck. "How he almost dived for the net one time when a big Daddy Longlegs crawled up his arm? I thought he was a goner for sure. Us, too. Remember, Tina?"

"Eddy's no fool; he wouldn't have jumped." Beside me, Tina lit a cigarette. She took a long drag and exhaled. "Anyway, that was years ago." Sighing, she exclaimed, "It'll be a heart attack that gets him, what with all that weight he's put on."

"You got that right," agreed Darla.

They fell silent then, but having them near me dug up other memories. Like the time we performed out in Saskatchewan. It was August. There'd been no air conditioning in that arena, and the whole place stunk of elephant shit. There'd been a slip-up, too. A tumble into the net, Eddy and Darla. Afterward, when the crowd had cleared, Eddy and I had sat alone on two hard seats just over an Exit sign, and drank warm ginger ale out of paper cups. He was morose and withdrawn, remembering his parents who'd both been killed. I remembered, too. Same town, years before. A bad fall, the net not secured properly. Eddy said that circus life sucked; that the first chance he had to get a regular

job, he was outta there. Couldn't see any sense in ending up a pile of
guts on some bloody rink floor like his mother and his old man.

And, true to his word, the very next week he did take off. Got
himself a factory job, standing all day operating a rivet gun. The circus
boss was hopping. Almost didn't take him on again. But after a week,
Eddy was back to swinging on those bars, more daring than ever. Said it
was the best life there was, feeling like you could fly.

Me, I was a different story. Taking up with the women. Bouts of
unhappiness at the transient lifestyle. Like the times I got fed up and
thought about raising chinchilla, growing tomatoes, opening a tattoo
shop. And then there were the other times when I loved the circus.
Those late summer nights, sitting outside my tin trailer, watching the
stars, listening to the animals shuffling, to Fern snoring two doors
down, to someone getting lucky. To that crazy, motley, surrogate family
that had raised me, taken me everywhere. On a gypsy vacation that
never ended.

"So, Roddy," Tina said as we pulled up to the fairgrounds, "don't be a
stranger. I left a schedule with Eddy. Bring him around sometime to see
the show." And Darla gave me a playful punch on the arm, and whispered
from the back seat, "We'll be here another three nights," and then they
were out of the car. Two graceful, aging redheads slipping away arm in
arm toward a huddle of forlorn travel trailers. A sliver of moon in the
black sky. Jungle scents in the air. I felt a twinge in my heart.

* * *

"I was taking a bath and alls I heard was a high, high sound,
halfways between a scream and a madman's roar, and then this terrible
thud." Prissy explaining after I'd returned. "For a minute, I thought it
was Fern, having nightmares and fallen out of her bed." She glanced
distractedly at Fern, whose flowered kimono was on inside out. We were
all standing at the top of the cellar steps. "And then," Prissy went on in
a voice still shaky, "I heard this laugh. So I climbed out of the tub, and I
ran down to see what was happening, because by now I knew it wasn't
Fern, and the cellar door was open and there he was, all spread out on

the floor, his head cracked open, and the weirdest noises coming out of him." Prissy stopped to catch her breath. "And all of a sudden, he stopped moving, and I saw his eyes roll back in his head." She slapped her rashy cheeks.

The space down there was empty now. Only a pool of red remained, shiny under the glare of a single dangling bulb. The ambulance had taken him away before I'd gotten back. I felt sick, and my knees started to tremble. All the close calls, all the risks we'd endured over the years now marched through my head. I wanted to yell at him, grab him by the shoulders and shake him for being so selfish and so stupid. I wanted to wipe out this night.

Instead, I went back for Tina and Darla. Not surprisingly, I found them still up, smoking. Scattered across their tiny table were a few dozen hundred dollar bills. "What do you make of this?" With a pained face, Darla read from Eddy's letter, "I'll be waiting on our high wire in the sky."

* * *

And so we buried him, after a full circus funeral. There was Phoenix in her tiara and hoop earrings and bangles; all the animal trainers in their best show garb; Trixie and Tawny, the other trick riders; even Vladimir the magician. Soaky the clown and his three sidekicks ushered, in full clown attire. Prissy sang, and Phoenix assisted the minister in proclaiming that Eddy's spirit had gone to heaven. Fern used up a whole box of Kleenex, and I sat in the second pew behind Darla and Tina and stared at the hymn book in the little shelf at my knees.

"Here's a challenge for you now, Vladimir," I said glumly to the old Russian outside the chapel, as we waited for the circus bus to take us all out to the graveyard. "Show us your stuff. Bring him back to life."

"Vish I could." Vladimir's small black eyes held none of their usual fire. "Vish I could."

* * *

So, out of our bunch, there's just me left here in Tiggleston now. I'm renting a small apartment over top the store. Fern is in a nursing home twenty miles away, after having a stroke which left her right side paralyzed. She is down to about a hundred and ninety pounds, God bless her soul, and every time I go and see her I call her Beautiful. She likes that and winks from her good eye, and we laugh. Prissy got married to a farmer she met down in the hotel. She's raising Welsh ponies in her old age. Sometimes I drive out, and we have a meal around their big harvest table, me and her and Charlie, and then we go to the barn and she shows me Rufus, her prize white stallion. "Spittin' image of old Aladdin, isn't he?" And her face softens as she remembers her favourite circus pony.

Mostly I get up early these days. It's spring again and I like to take a walk along the road just as the sun is coming up. The air is still nippy, but the robins are busy pulling up worms from the dewy grass, and the village is quiet. Just past the last house and a turn in the road is the little cemetery where we put Eddy. A small, flat white stone, unmarked. There was some fuss between Darla and Tina as to what should be engraved on it, so for now, or forever, it's plain. They'd wanted him buried out west, alongside their parents, but Eddy had picked this place. It was all in the note. He said he'd walked along here that last summer and felt it was as good a place as any to end up in, underneath those maples in the far corner. I couldn't imagine Eddy taking this walk, but he must have. He must have snuck around on his trips to the store, done some investigating, for he'd paid for a plot.

And when I round the curve and come upon the cemetery, often the sun is flickering through the branches of the trees. And it's like the wink of a tiara, the flash of bangles, or the glitter of a trapeze outfit. Always catching your eye. A bit of circus dazzle.

THE TROUBLE WITH SAINTS

My statue of St. Francis has never been replaced, but the village is as I remember: more prosperous now that its villas, once occupied by Mussolini's bureaucrats, have been restored to a benevolent self-confidence. Tourists eat ice-cream in the central café, but the local men still argue in the bar further down Lake Garda, near the smaller port where I first kissed Emanuela.

St. Francis was a few cobbled streets away, a larger version of those figures found in shops for religious kitsch. He stood in a brightly-lit shrine, eyes cast down and hand raised in blessing. Each night, after taking Emanuela home, I'd lay at his feet a pink flower from the bushes. Now I look at the empty niche thinking I'm the only one who knows why he's no longer there.

I'd talk to him of Emanuela — even, occasionally, of Clara. But it was to Emanuela that I'd say "I love you," as she rested her head on my shoulder, looking at me with brown eyes and whispering *mio caro*. The knowledge that somewhere she had a husband gave our love greater poignancy.

"No one knows I'm married," she told me that first night as we listened to the waves in the darkness, while my hand stroked her nipples inside her dress. "My father couldn't have trusted me if he'd known I'd married someone who wore a Fascist uniform."

The war had been over for two years, and I wandered across Northern Italy justifying my search for adventure with journalistic pretensions, sending articles to editors in Toronto. It was Emanuela's father I'd come to interview, and my article about him was the only one I'd sell. A prosperous winemaker, he'd joined the Italian underground when he was fifty, using his villa for meetings under the nose of Mussolini, then ruling his collapsing empire from nearby Salò. But because of his shyness and my imperfect Italian, our first meeting hadn't been a success. "Mister Tony, could you return the day after tomorrow? Tonight, I go to Milan."

He'd been telling me of a cheap *pensione* when his daughter came in: a mischievous Botticelli nymph with impudent eyes. "Emanuela," he turned to her, "please accompany our guest to the door."

"He likes you," she told me as she showed me out. "Don't be put off by his awkwardness." Her hand lingered in my own as she looked into my eyes.

"Could you..." I began, aware that our bodies were almost touching, "could you...help by telling me about your father, too?"

"Of course," she said, and we agreed to meet that afternoon.

But the Pensione Flora didn't have a room until two nights later. I left my suitcase there and went hunting, but by four o'clock I still hadn't found anywhere I could afford.

"I can invite you to the villa, then," Emanuela said in the newly-opened café by the harbour. "Maria — she's our maid — won't mind; she'll just grumble as always."

I looked at this delightfully brazen girl in front of me, thinking how she might make up for my disappointment with Clara.

So we met again that evening. Impatient to kiss each other, we walked along by the lake. Then, taking my hand, she told me about her husband. There'd been only a clandestine honeymoon before Alberto, after Italy's capitulation, had been mobilized by the Germans. Near

Ortona, he'd been taken prisoner, but had later escaped. That was all she knew.

"I can't tell anyone, I can't marry again. I have to pretend I've never been...intimate with a man."

We walked back to the villa, and each time we kissed I had to awkwardly put down my briefcase, in which I had my toothbrush and pyjamas. "What are you doing fooling around with pyjamas?" she asked.

As we made love in her bed that night, she was an extraordinary mixture of provocativeness and self-doubt. Next morning, waking early, she turned on her radio, stretching across me so that her breasts brushed over my lips. It was a programme of classical music, some of Grieg's *lieder* with their swelling crescendos, and I eased myself into her as the piano led into his famous "I love you." I translated the words as Emanuela moved her hips beneath me: "I love you, in time and eternity."

But after two nights her father returned and I had to move to the Pensione Flora. She couldn't risk coming to me there, so now we could only kiss passionately on our bench in the darkness.

"Help us to be together," I'd pray to St. Francis after I'd left her: explaining that I wasn't traditionally religious and that churches and saints were important in my life only because, if one's interested in Italian art, they're unavoidable.

* * *

In those days, I dreamed of becoming a great lover, but it never turned out that way. I'd recently dreamt of love with Clara, which now embarrassed me. How could I have imagined it, when her commitment was to God alone?

I'd met her in Padua, where I was staying in a Hotel Agape, named appropriately for Christian rather than erotic love. I was standing in St. Antony's Basilica beside his sarcophagus built into an enormous altar.

"He'll grant your request; I guarantee it."

I turned to see this dark-haired girl: a Tiepolo cherub, I thought. I started to object that I wasn't one of the usual pilgrims, but was there only because the Chapel with the Giotto frescoes was closed. But, looking at her smile and dark locks of hair, I stammered: "I guess he's my patron saint."

She indicated that we should line up behind the black-shawled women waiting to touch the sarcophagus, which was covered with letters giving thanks for favours received. To me it seemed miracle enough that I'd been spared the effort of myself approaching an attractive girl, so I too, feeling foolish, said a prayer of thanks, watching as her lips moved in silent devotion.

"So your name's Antonio?" she asked me over coffee.

"Tony, yes."

"Mine's Clara, Clara Gentile. Can you imagine a nicer name?"

It suited her: kind, pleasant, gentle.

"One day God will call you," she insisted. "I guarantee it."

I had no desire to be called by God, but to talk about religion seemed the obvious way to get to know her.

As she led me around medieval Padua, she told me her only passion was to see Christ in his second coming, assuring me this would be soon.

"And will people recognize him?"

"Absolutely. Because he'll come in glory. And I know I'll see him: either in my lifetime or at the moment of my death."

Strolling through cobbled streets, by the market with its thirteenth-century Palazzo della Ragione, she talked of her guardian angel. Believing I was an unconscious pilgrim — I laughed at that! — she showed me almost every church, always stopping for a prayer. But she had a sense of fun and showed no disapproval when I argued that one should enjoy worldly pleasures too.

"I'll pray for you," Clara laughed. "You'll come to God; I guarantee it."

She invited me to dinner the next evening. She had only two rooms and a miserable kitchen, their walls covered with religious paintings. I learned she was a teacher, giving most of what she earned to the church. But whenever I tried asking about her personal life, she kept returning to her religion — and to the Pope, whose every utterance, she maintained, reflected God's truth. In vain I argued about the

Concordat with Nazi Germany and Pius XII's pro-German attitudes during the war. "He had to choose between terrible alternatives," she defended him. "At least, the Fascists stood up to the evil of Communism!"

So she'd given a grudging assent to Mussolini. The resistance fighters, she explained, had been duped by the Communists. Her brother was one: "He's given me so many problems. My conversion to Catholicism caused a rift between us." Before I could ask about the conversion, she continued: "Of course, the Fascists betrayed us. But we're told to love our enemies."

I disagreed with her views but she argued charmingly, refusing to judge others: "Only God can do that."

When, unwisely, I tried to kiss her she dodged me, and we parted laughing.

I returned several times. Her cooking was abominable, which I don't think she even realized. Irritated by her unquestioning belief, I found her attractive just the same. Perhaps, I suggested, she was the only saint I'd ever met. She made a joke of it: "All I need is credit for a few miracles!"

St. Antony, Clara told me, was a disciple of St. Francis, so when a few weeks later I came upon my statue I was again reminded of her. I'd left Padua disappointed, finding that I could never really get close to her. She'd never speak of herself except in terms of her faith, and nor could I talk sincerely about my own deepest longings because, while accepting them, she saw them as failings to be prayed about. It was as though there were indeed a guardian angel standing beside Clara, who perhaps had the radiance of God but it set her apart from other mortals.

When I told St. Francis about this, he only winked, saying we all had different purposes in life.

And that very day, I met Emanuela. I plunged into my affair with her all the more recklessly, finding the abandon that love demanded, our bodies moistening for each other at the slightest touch. But after I took up residence in the *pensione* we knew all the passion of despair. October became November, and we had to dress more warmly for our bench, hands stretching under more layers to caress those enticing places we longed for. If we brought each other to a climax, I had a cold and clammy walk home, with St. Francis laughing at my discomfort as I stood before him.

"Help us to find a way," I begged him, while he gazed down inscrutably.

Emanuela's father soon came to approve of me — for I was a Canadian, one of the allies — and one evening he invited me to dinner.

"He hopes...you might want to marry me," she said. "But what can I do? For my marriage to come out...I couldn't hurt him that way."

He stammered during the meal, apologizing for not inviting me earlier because of his difficulties since his wife had died. Afterwards, he reached for a leather-bound book.

"D'Annunzio," Emanuela said: "Reading poetry's his way of sharing with his friends."

He was embarrassed. "To help you...write about the paradox of the Italians that led to Fascism. Eh?"

My Italian wasn't up to understanding poetry. But as he read, I couldn't help being moved by the flowing, musical cadences.

"Yet Gabriele D'Annunzio, who created such beauty," he paused, "wanted to be a hero, wanted glory. To wield the sword as well as the pen: 'Not to plot, but to dare,' he wrote."

Emanuela giggled. "And that he didn't know which pleased him most, to spill blood or to spill sperm!"

Her father chuckled to hide his embarrassment. "Violence, sensuality, decadence, heroism. Fine in poetry, but..." He was interrupted by the door-bell. "Maria's in the kitchen; get it will you please, Emanuela?" He went on: "But when it comes to life around you...eh? It's easy to blame the Germans, but Italians, too..."

Emanuela returned and handed me a telegram. "Forgive me for opening it. Your name didn't show in the window."

I read the words "TONY PLEASE COME CLARA" — sent to the only address I'd been able to give her.

"How many others are there?" Emanuela asked as she showed me out.

When Clara met me in Padua, I walked by without recognizing her, and she had to run after me. She wore a scarf over her head, but the shining black locks were gone. So too, I realized, was the rest of her hair.

"Why, why didn't you come as soon as you got my telegram?" she sobbed.

I hadn't realized how important it was. Few people had telephones then, and I hadn't been able to talk to her. By the time Emanuela had come to an unwilling acceptance of my irrational feeling that I should do as Clara asked, it was too late for the last bus. I could only send a telegram saying I'd arrive the next evening. But it wasn't the loss of Clara's hair that I'd have prevented.

"Last night," Clara told me, "I...was raped."

She led me through those familiar streets, crossing herself each time we passed a church, walking so fast that I couldn't ask what had happened. Not until we reached her apartment did she start to talk, her tears dripping onto a plate of spaghetti she'd prepared for me but had let boil so long it was barely edible.

"Tony, I must tell you something. I'm Jewish."

She took off her scarf, revealing only a slight stubble covering her scalp. I might have guessed it, but I never think about such things.

"I changed my name. To something I liked better."

Choosing Gentile, I thought, with all the solemnity of a sacrament. Of course: Italian for both 'gentle' and 'gentile.'

"It was during the occupation. My parents were deported. My brother Giuseppe attributed it to cowardice. It wasn't cowardice, I swear! I was safe: hidden by Catholic priests. It was then that I saw God, became converted."

I was impatient to know what had happened, but she needed to tell me in her own way, crying the whole time. It had started three days

151

before, when Giuseppe had come to see her and they'd got into an argument about his Communism.

"I don't even know why I bothered with him! How could I ever make him understand my opposition to the forces of the Antichrist?!"

"Finally, he'd stormed out in anger, but had returned later with some friends.

"I shouldn't have let them in, but I couldn't cast aside my own brother! They'd been drinking. Called me a Nazi, accused me of betraying my parents. Then they shaved my head." She ran her hands over the stubble. "But that," she sobbed, "was nothing, just vanity! The next day, at mass, I met this student I know, Enrico. When I told him what they'd done, he hardened his heart. He told his friends: some of them Christians, but some...well neo-Fascists, too. All they could think of was revenge and what weapons they could get hold of. 'Love your enemies,' I kept saying to them, but they wouldn't listen. That's when I sent you the telegram. An outsider...they'd have respected you." Clara shook her bald head with quiet despair. "Last night, you didn't come. I knew they were planning to find Giuseppe and his friends: they used to fight at school, too. I was afraid someone would get killed because of me! And they were Christians!

"I didn't know what to do. Find them and stop them, or not get involved, which was cowardly. Yet after an hour in prayer I felt God had heard me and I could leave it to Him. Only then I started wondering what might be happening. 'Beware of vain curiosity,' we're told: if only I'd heeded that! Instead, I decided to go to Giuseppe's and find out."

Where, Clara, I thought, was your guardian angel?

"A voice kept telling me 'Go back,' but I wanted to find out. Curiosity was my sin, and how God punished me!"

She'd found about ten of them at her brother's apartment, and there was blood everywhere. But it turned out to have come mostly from a nosebleed. There'd been a brawl; then, honour satisfied, they'd got into Giuseppe's stock of wine.

"Nothing terrible had happened, and I could only kneel and pour out my gratitude." She smiled as though still remembering to be thankful, then started crying again. "Lord, do with me according to Your good pleasure, and do not reject my sinful life."

I took her hand, happy at least to appear in the role of comforter.

"But the fighting had excited them, they were...proud of themselves. Wanting to glorify in their sin, do something worse. My praying made them more excited, and I realized they were looking at me with lust. Even Enrico. They started taunting me, trying to get me to drink, and when I wouldn't they grabbed me, pushed me to the floor, stuck the bottle into my mouth so I had to swallow or be choked. 'This is my blood which was given for thee,' I heard Enrico — defiling the Blessed Sacrament! 'And this is my body,' came another voice. They had my legs apart, and I felt someone clawing at my underclothes and forcing himself into me. All I could do was shut my eyes and keep from choking on the wine they kept pouring into my mouth."

For once, I thought, she was speaking about herself, but with detachment, as though she'd rehearsed the words.

"After a while I remember thinking that it didn't hurt so much, although I knew I must be bleeding. They...took me in turns. And...after a while it didn't seem so bad. I could observe it all and think Madonna, this is happening to me!"

I was silent, uneasy.

"In the past, I'd denied myself so much," she went on. "It was terrible, but there was even a curiosity within me, to know what it was like, can you imagine? Then they weren't holding me down. I remember sitting up and taking off my clothes to keep them from being torn or getting more blood on them — knowing it was an excuse, that I wasn't really concerned about them. I knew I should be in despair, but part of me...I can only put it like this...was enjoying my shame and humiliation. 'Blessed are ye when men shall revile you,' I was thinking. I was proud that I was a martyr, and that none of it was my fault! Only it began to change. I began to do everything they suggested, terrible things. Not from pleasure, I don't even know why, perhaps just to be able to say I'd done them. Things I thought I'd driven from my imagination by prayer and fasting."

"You're only human."

"Alas," she quoted from somewhere, "a perverted pleasure overcomes the mind that counts it a delight to lie among the brambles." She looked at me with defiance. "Giuseppe was the last, his lips bleeding as he kissed my neck, my breasts, even my..." She indicated with her hand. "Then he seemed to stay inside me forever. Now I'm damned, I thought. Now I know Satan. I didn't care. My own brother!"

* * *

That night, on her sofa, I was torn between thoughts of what had happened and, I admit it, a newly aroused eroticism, a desire to make love to her myself: gently, happily. Clara in the next room was wakeful, too. But I was betrayed by my own timidity. Not wanting her to think I was like those others, I didn't even show the natural affection that might have helped both of us.

I returned to the village feeling guilty. Yet as the bus skirted Lake Garda, taking me past D'Annunzio's ornate villa, I knew it was Emanuela I wanted — that Clara represented for me Christian love, agape, while it was the pagan eros I longed for.

I'd rarely stopped to talk to St. Francis in daytime. But now I needed to compose my mind. I had another problem, too: my money was running out. Should I do the logical thing and return to Canada, or prolong an impossible situation with Emanuela?

St. Francis promised to find a solution to my dilemma, and I walked to the villa telling myself to expect a miracle.

Emanuela answered the door, kissed me, looked at me with those mysterious eyes, then led me into the living-room. "My husband's alive."

"You've seen him?"

"He's in prison. He sent a message to my father! I had to tell him everything! Alberto's coming out and needs somewhere to go."

It seemed like a bad melodrama, and I barely restrained a desire to laugh.

"Alberto's a petty crook! He ran away from the Americans with one of their soldiers, and lived by the black market. He never bothered to come back!"

"And you?"

"I'm married to him. You know what that means in Italy?"

She could see nothing but emptiness for us ahead. "All we have is physical. There's not even a way to sleep together."

Her father, when I said goodbye, shook his head. "Eh, Mr. Tony. I'm sorry, eh? I'd have been happy...but how could I have known? Eh!"

It was dark when I reached our bench, where I sat listening to the waves. Then I walked to where St. Francis was waiting. "Thanks! You were going to answer my prayer."

"I did," he said. "You asked me to find a solution."

"That's not the way I wanted! You were no fucking use!"

Still, he gazed down at an earthenware pot in which someone had arranged some of the flowers.

I've never been a violent man, able to spill blood: spilling sperm is more in my line, although if truth be known I've spilt little enough of that in my wretched life. But, faced now with emptiness, I could only indulge in futile gestures.

I took the pot, dumped the flowers and, infuriated at the mocking radiance of his face, thrust the pot against it. The statue didn't have the inner strength I imagined. A crack appeared in one shoulder, darted across the body and slowly head, torso and raised arm slid down, then toppled to the ground, breaking into several pieces.

I was both dismayed and elated. I started grabbing the pieces, throwing them down in a fever of destruction; toppling the statue's base so that it too shattered onto the road. The light in the niche went out. I was horrified, but I couldn't stop, throwing the larger pieces at St. Francis' eyes, nose, lips: crunching my heel on the slivers I reduced them to.

I heard later that Clara had become a nun. She wrote assuring me that she prayed for me, and I hadn't the heart to reply that it didn't seem to help during my troubled professional years. Six months ago, her

Mother Superior wrote instead, saying Clara had died from cancer, that she'd been loved for her saintliness, and that "She had the radiance of God." Did she see Christ in his glory at the moment of her death?

I'd been thinking of returning to Italy ever since the break-up of my marriage. With no more dreams of becoming a great lover, I'd be happy to settle for one woman to love. With the tourists, I eat ice-cream in the café, reading about atrocities committed by the Red Brigade. At night, I sit on my bench, listening to the waves, thinking that Emanuela must be out there somewhere. Then I walk to her father's villa, ring the bell, but the house is as empty as the shrine where the statue once stood.

I go to find it, hoping that St. Francis miraculously will be there. But there's nothing except the empty niche and the pink flowers.

Tomorrow I'll go to Padua, to the Basilica of St. Antony where, with the believers, I'll line up to touch the sarcophagus. Perhaps I'll pray to Clara.

Clara, Clara, please send me a miracle: I beg you with this stupid heart of mine! I'd like to have believed; why deny it? All you need is credit for one miracle, so I can pray to you. Not that I may find Emanuela, it's too late for that, I don't deserve it, but that one day, there'll be someone to love again.

About the Authors

SYLVIA
ADAMS

Ottawa, ON. Her novel, *This Weather of Hangmen*, was published in 1996. Her work has appeared in *Arc, The New Quarterly, Symbiosis* and three League of Canadian Poets anthologies. She has won *Seeds* 1998 International Poetry competition, the Valley Writers' Guild *Joker is Wild* contest for humorous poetry — twice — the CAA National Capital Region contest for free verse — twice — and their non-fiction contest in 1995. Her poetry collection, *Mondrian's Elephant*, was the 1998 Cranberry Tree Chapbook contest winner. In 1997, she received the CAA's Don Thomson award.

JEAN
BARNARD

Victoria, BC. She was raised and educated in the farm community of Fairy Glen, Saskatchewan, and has taken a variety of university and community college courses. Jean worked in banks and office jobs while accompanying her husband on military postings across Canada, the United States and Western Europe. They operated their own electronics business at North Bay, Ontario, for seventeen years, then moved to Victoria, BC, for retirement living. Jean has been published in *The Shield, Der Kanadier, The Lowthair* and *The Kapuskasing Consumer Guides* — all little newspapers. She is an active member of the Victoria and Islands Branch and editor of the *Victoria Calling* newsletter. She is writing a novel and more short stories.

JANET BLACHFORD

Montreal, QC. She has made occasional forays to Toronto and elsewhere. She is married and has two sons and a daughter, all adults now. Her education includes a BA and MA in English from McGill University, and some teaching experience there. Recently, she started a PhD program, also at McGill, but rapidly discovered that writing fiction was again the greener field. She continues to work at unpublished novels and assorted short stories, and agrees with everyone who thinks that writing is the most satisfactory way to spend a day — or a lifetime.

YVONNE BLACKWOOD

Markham, ON. She was born in Jamaica and immigrated to Canada in 1976. She is a Community Banking Advisor with the Royal Bank of Canada and has been a Banker for twenty-seven years. Yvonne began her writing career in 1997 after an intriguing journey to West Africa. She has published two short stories with another due out this fall. As Director of Marketing for the CAA, Metro Branch, she writes monthly articles for the *Author's Newsletter*. She is the editor for a job related newsletter, *Financial Focus*, and a columnist for *Pride News Magazine*. Yvonne is currently seeking a publisher for her book, *Into Africa*. She has two children, Michele and Robert and two grand children, Eliza and Monroe.

BILL CROWELL

South Ohio, NS. Following a career of teaching Art and English, he moved with his wife, Fran, to Lake Annis: a summer cottage village four miles beyond the pavement in Yarmouth County, Nova Scotia. He spends part of his time in painting and part in writing, and does not know how he ever found time for "real" work. Previous publications include a number of short stories, some non-fiction and two novels.

MARGARET DEEFHOLTS

Surrey, BC. Of Anglo-Indian parentage, she was born and grew up in India, emigrating to Canada with her family in 1977. She began her writing career in 1994 and has won various Canadian magazine short fiction awards since then. While several of her stories are set in India and explore the lives and cultural diversity of its people, Margaret also writes about the dichotomies which confront first and second generation Indo-Canadians who live in Surrey and Vancouver.

In addition to short fiction, Ms. Deefholts' articles on her travels through Canada, Britain, Europe, Australia and India, have been published in BC Magazines and community newspapers throughout the Lower Mainland. She is currently working on a book-length narrative relating to her life and journeys in India.

DELIA
De SANTIS

Brights Grove, ON. She was born in Italy and came to Canada at age thirteen. She is married and has two grown sons. Her short stories have won awards and have appeared in many literary magazines, including *Zymergy, The First Person, Pleiades, Nutshell Quarterly* and *The Prairie Journal*, and the anthologies: *Flare Up, Sands of Huron, Voices of the Rapids, The Anthology of Italian Canadian Writing* and *Pillars of Lace*.

JUNE
FROST

Tiverton, ON. She has short stories in *Wordscape* 3, 4 and 7 — metro Toronto branch anthologies. In 1999, her work appeared in *The Brucedale Family Reader* and *Legion Magazine*. She was delighted to receive an honourable mention in the CAA collection *Winners' Circle 5*, to win *The White Water Journal* skinny dipping contest in 1998, The Brucedale Press 1995 humour contest and *The Sun Times* 1994 Holiday competition. She lives and writes within view of Lake Huron in Bruce County, Ontario.

M. JENNIE
FROST

Edmonton, AB. She is a professional storyteller. She has performed at public festivals, conferences, and in schools in her hometown and also in Lethbridge, Vancouver, Winnipeg and Toronto. She is a member of TALES — The Alberta League Encouraging Storytelling — and of Storytellers of Canada/Conteurs du Canada as well as CAA. Jennie also writes poetry and is an enthusiastic member of Edmonton's Stroll of Poets. She has had seven poems published in journals and anthologies. "Space" is her first published story.

DONNA
GAMACHE

MacGregor, MA. Donna Gamache is a writer and substitute teacher. She specializes in fiction for both adults and children, but also publishes short poetry and occasional non-fiction. Her children's novel, *Spruce Woods Adventure*, was published in 1994 by Compascor Manitoba. She has been published in Canada and the US, in such diverse publications as *Cricket*, *Highlights for Children*, *The Friend*, *Guide*, *Our Family*, *Western People*, and the *Toronto Sunday Star*. One story was recently republished in Sweden. She has won awards in contests by the *Toronto Star* and the Canadian Authors Association (Manitoba), and won the Metropolitan Toronto CAA *Winners' Circle 6* contest. She is presently working on several other book manuscripts for children and young adults.

She has been a member for many years of CAA, the Manitoba Writers' Guild and a local writing group, Prairie Pens. When not reading,

writing or teaching, Donna enjoys travelling, camping, bicycling and cross-country skiing with her
husband, Luc. They have three grown sons.

KERRY LYNN
PARSONS

Lakefield, ON. She is a graduate of Trent, Queen's
and the Universite' de Nantes in France; primarily,
she writes plays, poetry and short stories. Four of
her plays have had public performances and several poems have been published. Kerry Lynn is currently President of the Peterborough branch of the
CAA, a Friend of CANSCAIP and a member of
IWWG. She teaches school and also enjoys garden-
ing, golf, badminton, cross-country skiing and
cycling. Kerry Lynn has lived and travelled abroad,
but home is a country cottage in the heart of the
Kawarthas, with Bailey and Casey, where she is
currently working on a drama book and two plays.

SHEILA
PAYNTER

Westbank, BC. Born in Kelowna, BC, in 1920, Sheila
attended Peachland's three room school for twelve
years. After receiving her Arts BA from UBC during
WWII, she worked as a fitter's helper for Dominion
Bridge and joined the RCAF. She married and had
six children. She is published in *Okanagan Diary*
in *B.C. Farmer and Gardener*, as well she has self-
published three books with an outdoor focus: *First
Time Around, Reflections on the Lake*, and
Okanagan Golf Points of View. Presently, she is
writing a monthly column for *Westside Weekly*.

BRUCE
SMITH

Burlington, ON. Bruce was raised in Jamaica, and went to boarding school at de Carteret School in Mandeville, Jamaica and Ridley College, St. Catharines, ON. Later, he attended Quaker meetings in Hamilton and became a social activist joining BAND — Burlington Association for Nuclear Disarmament —, Jubilee 2000 to forgive Third World debt, and the Green Party, as well as contesting the Burlington riding in the last provincial election. When diagnosed with multiple sclerosis recently, his teaching duties in an Ontario public school for twenty-five years came to an end. He is a divorced father of two children.

JOAN
TOVENATI

Beamsville, ON. She was born in Wales, but now lives in the Niagara Peninsula. Her poetry has appeared in several anthologies, including *The Harpweaver*, Brock University and *Vintage 97/98*, The League of Canadian Poets. "My Sarah at Ninety" was short-listed in The Writers' Union of Canada Postcard Story Competition, 1999, and her short story, "The Dinner Bag," was shortlisted in their Short Prose Competition for Developing Writers Contest, 1998. Her story, "Waiting," won the fiction award in *The Amethyst Review*, May 1998. Other short stories have been in *Kairos 9*, Niagara Branch's Short Fiction Group's three anthologies and others. She has recently completed her first novel.

DIANNE
WEY

Neustadt, ON. Her short stories have appeared in numerous publications, including *Green's Magazine, The Grand Table, Western People,* and *Quarry.* In 1996, HMS Press published a collection of her short fiction, *Country Hearts,* electronically. A former office worker, she now lives with her husband on a farm in south-western Ontario. She has two sons from a previous marriage.

A. COLIN
WRIGHT

Kingston, ON. He is professor emeritus of Russian Studies at Queen's University, and has published many articles on Russian and comparative literature, including a major book on Mikhail Bulgakov. His stories have appeared in various Canadian and British literary magazines: *Dalhousie Review, Descant, Event, Green's Magazine, Journal of Canadian Fiction, Nebula, NeWest Review, New Quarterly, paperplates, Quarry, Scrivener, Storyteller Magazine, Waves, Stand Magazine.* He also writes novels and plays; he was the 1993 winner in the Special Merit Category of Theatre BC's National Playwriting Competition for his stage adaptation of *Lieutenant Kizhe,* subsequently performed at Kingston's Theatre 5.

GILLIAN
M. FOSS

Ottawa, ON. She is an award-winning writer/editor with *Reader's Digest* among her clients. She has been a CAA Regional Vice President, Chair of the CAA Literary Awards Committee for four years, and currently is CAA's National President. She has programmed two national writers' conferences and teaches as a subject specialist for a consulting company.

BERNICE
LEVER

Richmond Hill, ON. She was editor for fifteen years of the award-winning literary journal, *WAVES*. For over three decades, she has been a CAA member and worker as well as coordinator of the Richvale Writers Club. A Seneca College English professor, she was the Metropolitan Toronto CAA's branch's Writer's-in-Residence, 1998/1999. Her grammar textbook, *The Colour of Words*, will soon become a website resource. Also a member of The League of Canadian Poets, Bernice has published six books of poetry, such as *Things Unsaid*, 1996, and *Uncivilizing*, 1997, and is arranging her *New and Selected Poems*, Black Moss, 2000.